THE TREE OF LIFE:

STORIES OF CIVIL WAR

by

Mario Bencastro

Translated by
Susan Giersbach Rascón

Arte Público Press
Houston, Texas
1997

This volume is made possible through grants from the National Endowment for the Arts (a federal agency), Andrew W. Mellon Foundation, the Lila Wallace-Reader's Digest Fund and the City of Houston through The Cultural Arts Council of Houston, Harris County.

Recovering the past, creating the future

Arte Público Press
University of Houston
Houston, Texas 77204-2090

Cover design by Vega Design Group

Bencastro, Mario.
    [Arbol de la vida. English]
    The tree of life and other stories / by Mario Bencastro.
       p.   cm.
    ISBN 1-55885-186-0 (trade paper. : alk. paper)
  I. Title.
  PQ7539.2.B46A813   1997
  863—dc21   96-49351
                                                   CIP

THE TREE OF LIFE:

STORIES OF CIVIL WAR

In memory of
María Magdalena Enríquez,
José Valladares Pérez,
Marianella García Villas,
Herbert Anaya,
Segundo Montes.

(1980-1990)

Table of Contents

CLOWN'S STORY

It's hard being a clown these days, especially since the country is in the midst of a civil war. People live thinking about death and have forgotten how to laugh.

Yesterday very few people came to the circus. But it was still an exceptional day. There was a political demonstration in the plaza at the time of our first show. Some people were standing at the entrance; they couldn't decide whether to come to the circus or join the demonstration. I was singing:

"A couple playing soccer
put on quite a show!
The old lady bent over
and the old man scored a goal!"

But the crowd in the plaza was shouting:

"The people! united!
will never be defeated!
The people! united!
will never be defeated!"

Their shouts were loud and persistent. It seemed absurd to see a clown doing somersaults looking like he was shouting political slogans instead of the usual jokes. Those who came to see the circus asked for their money back, saying that it was ridiculous, that they couldn't hear anything, and they went away. The circus was left completely deserted. Even the employees went home, without bothering to ask for their pay because they knew it would be a waste of time. There wasn't a single penny in the till.

After a while the police arrived to break up the demonstration. In the plaza there was shooting and great confusion. Everyone ran amidst desperate screams, exploding bombs, and gunshots, trying to save themselves. I decided to close the circus. Several people managed to take refuge under the tents, but the police came and took them away. I was lucky they didn't arrest me. I sat quietly in a corner, with my painted face, wearing my baggy pants with bright colorful patches and my long yellow shoes, watching the police drag and club those who refused to obey the arrest orders.

"Clown, quit laughing!" said one of the policemen in a threatening voice. "This is no joke!"

I tried to explain to them that I wasn't laughing, that the makeup makes us clowns look happy even when we're sad, but the policeman came up to me and said, "I don't want to hear a word!"

I covered my face with my hands in their huge white gloves. Only after they had gone did I take my hands from my face - one finger at a time.

All that happened yesterday. The circus was closed for most of the day. And don't even mention the night. Darkness in San Salvador is not good for circuses, but it is good for other things, like arrests, assassinations, kidnappings, bombings, torture, macabre events which have nothing to do with the circus.

But, ladies and gentlemen, I've forgotten to introduce myself. I am Cachirulo; they call me "The Playful Clown." Really, I'm nothing special, let me tell you. I'm just like any ordinary circus artist. That is, I do sleight of hand and a few magic acts. Somersaults and juggling. I can jump through a ring of fire, and put my head into the jaws of a lion without getting bitten. I walk and run on the high wire, a routine act but a dangerous one because I do it without a safety net. If I lost my balance, I'd crash to the cement floor. I am also a trapeze artist and do the "leap of death." I can stand on one foot on the back of a running horse. I do the usual tricks of good circus professionals, but with the special attribute that I'm also a clown, which I dare say many consider the most difficult circus occupation.

I should clarify, ladies and gentlemen, that everything I know I learned from my father, who in his time was a great celebrity. His circus included many trained animals, like elephants, tigers, lions, monkeys, and horses. And of course he had a lot of employees, including a full band with excellent musicians. He had people with great talent for magic and the trapeze. Dwarves and giants. Tiger and lion tamers. Snake charmers. Even a fakir who would lock himself in a cage-a real hunger artist who once decided to show the world the full extent of his art. For several months he remained in his cage, motionless, without eating, drinking only a swallow of water each day. He won the admiration and respect of the audience. But he went on too long, to the point where the audiences and even the circus employees began to believe that he really was capable of going without eating for an indefinite time, and they forgot all about him. Seven months later they took him out of his cage, dead.

The circus was my father's life. He was an excellent clown of renowned talent. He received a decoration from the President of the Republic. I remember that in those days the circus travelled to all the important cities of Central America. Young and old waited for us with great excitement. Those were happy times for my father. Times he would remember with great nostalgia, that he would call "the golden age of the circus."

I not only learned everything from my father; I also inherited it all from him overnight. It happened in the middle of a show, while he was doing one of his famous magic acts. Suddenly he became petrified before the audience, which began to whistle with disapproval. Luckily, some clowns were ready to replace him and continue the performance, while I took my father by the arm and led him from the ring. I must have been about twenty years old and my father about forty. I still remember that moment. He looked at me with glassy eyes and smiled in a strange way, as if he were lost, absent. He did not recognize anyone nor did he say a word. A few days later he was put into the mental hospital.

I always visit him on Sundays. Although he completely lost his mind and ability to speak, he never stops smiling. The make-believe smile of his clown's makeup has remained painted on his face forever. In a way I think he's happy. And it seems to me that he always will be, as long as he doesn't know about the harsh reality our country is experiencing. As long as he doesn't stop smiling.

That's how the whole circus became mine. Animals, clowns, jugglers, trapeze artists, musicians, tents, trucks. Everything. I had always dreamed of having a circus like my father's, but I never imagined that I would inherit his, especially under such dramatic circumstances.

I think, though, that for him it was easy to be a clown. His were days of relative calm when people laughed easily. I remember seasons of steady attendance, when thousands of people waited in long lines, anxious to see the great spectacle the circus was then.

Mine, on the other hand, has been a very hard time. The country's economy is at rock bottom. A dark, sad era. A time of war when in order to survive I've had to let my fellow performers go. Many of them decided to leave on their own, recognizing that in the current situation people don't have the time or the money to watch and applaud clowns. I found out that an acrobat joined the guerrillas and a clown became a member of the National Guard. How absurd it would be if they faced each other in battle. Men who used to act in comedy together, now performing real tragedy, spilling each other's blood. Strange things. Matters of war.

Little by little I've had to get rid of the animals, too. Those I felt the worst about were the elephants. Because of the lack of food, they got so thin they looked like giraffes. I donated one of them to the zoo. The other died of starvation. The lions also had bad luck. One of them escaped during a battle which broke out in the plaza between rebels and security forces. The newspaper reported the event under the headline "Subversive Lion Shot to Death." The lioness also escaped from the circus. For a while she roamed the neighborhoods, causing terror with her roars and attacks. The newspaper reported the event with a lot of publicity: "Subversive Lion Comes Back to Life." But after a few days nothing further was heard about the animal. I was able to sell a pair of trained tigers to the zoo, where their antics brought great delight to young and old.

That's how I got rid of everything that was difficult to support. I had to give away the monkeys because they ate too much fruit. Along with them went a chimpanzee, to a man from Ahuachapán who said that he lived on a big farm that would be the perfect place for it. A few days later, I don't know how, the monkey returned to the circus. This animal was particularly valuable because it belonged to a species that was nearly extinct. Finally they came and took it to the zoo. A talking parrot is the only animal I have left. It's an old bird that every morning talks as though it were chatting with my father. Its food is simple and inexpensive. All it needs is a little cornmeal. I've been selling cages, benches, tents, and anything people are willing to buy.

In fact, right now I can see the truck arriving to pick up the last things I sold at auction prices, the last remains of the great circus that was my father's pride and joy.

For this occasion, in his honor, I have put on the clown costume he liked to wear for the big shows during happier days. As you can see, I have put on my tomato-red nose, my long yellow shoes, my baggy pants with colored patches, and a curly orange wig. I have also painted my face and drawn a big smile on it, because now that they are taking away the last of the circus I want to pretend to be happy, although this is really nothing other than the circus' funeral. But, ladies and gentlemen, I consider myself a good clown, and I'm not going to disappoint you by letting you see the tears that want to overflow because of this big lump of sadness in my throat.

I've decided that when they take everything away and all that remains of the circus is an empty space in the park, like a big shadow, I'm not going to cry, ladies and gentlemen; I promise you that I'm not going to shed a single tear. Like the good clown that I am, I'll tell you some jokes, do a couple of somersaults in the air, and then walk away with my parrot on my shoulder, my only possession and companion.

Ladies and gentlemen, I'll walk through these streets stained with blood and political slogans without looking back at the plaza where the circus performed for the last time. I'll travel through San Salvador, down every street of this destroyed city, until finally I find a child. And maybe when he sees this wandering clown, the child will smile, a wide, pure, innocent smile. Because then this story, though not such a happy one, would end with a smile. Because after all, ladies and gentlemen, it is a clown's story.

THE DEATHS OF
FORTÍN CORONADO

The confusion generated by the disappearance of Fortín Coronado is truly incredible. The newspapers publish extensive articles about the possible reasons for his death, more preposterous than yesterday's and surely less bold and complicated than tomorrow's.

They swear that a lover poisoned him out of jealousy.

They report that he was an agent of the intelligence service and that the insurgent forces executed him.

From the village of Plan de la Laguna, someone writes that he cultivated hallucinogenic mushrooms for export, became intoxicated, and that his corpse was found "hard as a rock."

In my neighborhood, the rumor is that Fortín Coronado was the owner of "The Little Panties," and that a young girl he had kidnapped from her parents in San Juan Nonualco and initiated into prostitution became disillusioned and stabbed him to death.

Others testify that he belonged to a clandestine organization and was mortally wounded in battle.

A well-known politician who holds a high position in the government, on the other hand, declared in a press conference:

"Fortín Coronado was my trusted friend. Those who slander me possibly assassinated him in order to accuse me of his death, since they constantly seek excuses to dirty my spotless reputation as chief guardian of the sacred public interest."

My grandmother, never one to be left out of these matters of national interest, says she knew him personally. According to her, when Fortín was still very young he made a deal with the devil and sold him his soul in exchange for a great fortune. But Lucifer, seeing that Fortín was gaining power too soon, moved up the agreed-upon date and carried him off to hell.

In short, everyone has something to say about the deceased. Maybe they feared, hated, or envied him so much that each one wants to kill him in his own way.

In the Municipal Mayor's Office the official death report is open to the public. But no one seems to take it seriously. According to the document:

"Fortín Coronado died while he slept, a natural death, of old age, and with a pleasant smile on his wrinkled face."

(1983)

THE INSATIABLE ONES

1

It was a hot afternoon and, as was his custom, the man was sitting in the wicker rocking chair reading the newspaper. He sat on the porch, facing the main road from town. On a table, within reach of his hand, the usual pitcher contained his favorite tamarind drink.

The alarming news made him think about how things were not like they used to be, "so much insurrection and violence now," he thought as he read the headlines GOVERNMENT INITIATES AGRARIAN REFORM, UNION LEADER DISAPPEARS, GUERRILLAS KIDNAP MILLIONAIRE, FACTORY BURNED AND BANK DYNAMITED, 10 DIE IN POLITICAL DEMONSTRATION, GOVERNMENT OFFICIAL MACHINE-GUNNED TO DEATH.

He finished reading at the exact moment that he was taking the last swallow of his drink. "It's my infallible knack for calculating time," he declared to his wife. He was unaware that she would slide very quietly behind the rocker and replace the empty pitcher with an identical full one, in order to have more time to meet the foreman of the plantation in the garden cottage next to the house. Age, or perhaps boredom, had made the old man forget his conjugal duties and his wife's young body.

At the same time every afternoon, a peddler would pass by on the road. From the iron gate he would hawk his wares. The old man would take his tired eyes off the newspaper and shout, "I've already told you I don't want anything, imbecile! Go sell your junk somewhere else!"

"Yes, sir, things have changed," he thought this time as he emptied the last glass. With great effort he got up and went off slowly in the direction of the bathroom, dragging his feet and holding his full stomach with both hands. After a long time he came out, zipping up his rumpled khaki pants. He sank into the armchair in the living room and called to his wife to turn on the television. It was time for his favorite soap opera.

2

The woman entered the living room after fixing her disheveled hair and adjusting her skirt. She turned on the television, sat down next to the old man and, as the program was beginning, caressed his gray head.

"Today Eduardo's going to show her the letters for sure," said the old man with some enthusiasm. "And maybe he'll throw her out of the house."

"No, he can't do that," objected the woman. "Victoria is his only company. Everyone has abandoned him since they found out that he has cancer and is going to die soon."

The name of the soap opera appeared on the screen as its dreamy, sad musical theme accompanied a voice which announced:

"Solimar Soap and Perfume, first in the care of your skin, presents the most acclaimed soap opera of all time, 'The Insatiable Ones,' starring Carlota San Martín in the unforgettable role of Victoria, and Juan Salomón Elcano as Eduardo, the best performance of his life."

"They changed the theme song," complained the woman with disgust. "And the new one is horrible."

"The man's voice sounds like a cat meowing," agreed the old man.

Victoria appeared on the screen and they fell silent. The scene showed Victoria facing a window which looked out on a garden, and behind her was a living room decorated with flowers, its walls full of mirrors and paintings of famous people, nude maidens and bullfighters in dazzling attire.

One of the living room doors opened suddenly and Eduardo, a man of advanced age but elegant appearance, entered. She turned and went toward Eduardo to embrace him, but he pushed her away and, in an angry voice, said:

"Victoria, this is the last straw! I never imagined you would betray me in such a low and cruel way!"

She, with poorly feigned surprise, looked him in the eye and answered:

"I don't know what you're talking about, my love."

Approaching her, he said disappointedly:

"After all I did for you. After I took you out of an orphanage and gave you a life full of riches."

The background music was heard, agitated and dizzying to denote suspense. The woman struck a malicious pose and, walking toward him with an exaggerated movement of her hips, responded:

"I don't have the faintest idea what you're referring to, my dear. Here I am, waiting for you, dying to see you, unable to sleep all night thinking about you, about us, and you come to me with..."

"I don't want to hear any more of your lies!" he said, interrupting her. "I found these letters, written to you by one of your lovers!"

Eduardo scornfully threw a fistful of letters onto a table and she, very nervous now, took one and read it. Her face took up the whole screen and showed expressions of surprise and concern.

"It can't be; this is slander! How can you distrust me and believe such lies! You know very well that you are the only man in my life!"

The scene was cut off abruptly by a commercial.

She stopped caressing the old man who, with his head resting on his chest, had fallen into a deep sleep. She got up slowly, tip-toed out of the living room, and disappeared behind a door. The foreman was waiting for her in a semi-dark corner and came to meet her, embracing her in the middle of the room and kissing her passionately, until she pulled away and said:

"No, not here."

"Why not?" asked the man anxiously. "The old man is asleep."

"No, he could wake up and discover us. Besides, the maid is around and you know what a gossip she is."

"Don't worry about her," said the man. "She has her fun with the other foreman."

He embraced her insistently. The theme song reached them and she could not help asking herself: "I wonder if Eduardo has left Victoria. Has he abandoned her?" Again she pulled away from him and said in a low voice:

"Not now. I said no! Come back tomorrow instead. He'll be gone to inspect the coffee harvest."

"Let's go to the garden cottage," he said, pulling her by the hand.

Incapable of resisting, she followed him and they disappeared through a door.

3

On another afternoon, when the old man had read several articles and had drunk his first glass of tamarind juice, as he was looking for the comics, he heard the voice of the peddler who, not satisfied with hawking his wares from the gate, came through it and stood right in front of him.

"Sir, buy something from me, even just a lottery ticket!"

"I've already told you I don't want anything, imbecile!" he exclaimed impatiently as he did every day. "Go sell your junk somewhere else!"

"Please, sir, buy something. Look at this precious piece of English cashmere; I'll give it to you cheap. It's a bargain, sir."

"Go to hell! Quit pestering me!"

"I haven't sold anything. I haven't eaten for three days! Don't be that way, sir; buy this magazine; can't you see I'm starving to death?"

"What do I care if you're starving to death? Instead of going around pestering people with your rubbish, go harvest coffee and then you'll have plenty of food."

"I also do magic and tell fortunes," said the peddler, imploring him. "Do you want me to tell yours, sir?"

He put his hands together as if to trap something and, when he opened them, a white dove emerged and flew off into the distance.

"That's just foolishness. Cheap tricks for ignorant people. I'm an attorney with a doctor's degree in law."

"It's true, believe me," insisted the peddler. "Just by looking into your eyes I can see that you held high positions in the government. Isn't that true, sir?"

"The whole world knows that," commented the old man, letting the newspaper fall to the ground.

"Yes, sir, you were Governor!" the peddler added without hesitation as he pointed to the ground with his index finger and made a pig appear.

For a moment the old man observed the nervous animal which went off grunting into the garden.

"Bah, everyone remembers that," he said proudly, taking a wad of bills out of his pocket and throwing him one. "Take this, buy yourself something to eat and leave me alone.

He caught the bill before it touched the ground. He took off his hat and threw it into the air. As it was coming down, the hat turned into a brightly colored bird and perched on the shoulder of the peddler who, after bowing to the old man who did not take his scornful gaze from him, picked up his bags and hurried off.

4

"Eduardo sure gave Victoria what she deserved," said the old man, sitting down in front of the television. "For being so evil. After he was so good to her."

"He's no saint either; he has his faults, too," said the woman in a defensive tone. "He cheated on her with the mayor's daughter. And don't forget the time he went on vacation to France with his secretary, that blonde I can't stand. I don't know what the hell Eduardo saw in her. He's so handsome he could win the most beautiful woman in the world."

"That happened because Victoria pretended to be sick," said the old man. "Just to go off to the country with one of her lovers."

"And what should she have done?" demanded the woman. "She can't spend all her time waiting for him locked up in that enormous mansion while he goes around Paris living it up with other women."

"But Eduardo took Victoria out of poverty and made her a lady of high society," said the old man, a bit worked up. "And it's so unfair for her to repay him like that."

"Well, don't get so excited; your blood pressure will go up again," she advised, sitting down next to him to caress his head. "Besides, it's only a soap opera and has nothing to do with real life."

The familiar theme song filled the living room and Victoria appeared on the screen, sitting on a wide sofa in the living room of a modern apartment. Alejandro, a handsome, stylishly-dressed young man, approached her and kissed her tenderly. She stood up and, in a desperate tone of voice, said:

"Eduardo has decided that we should separate."

"Who cares?" said the young man. "With all the money you'll get from the divorce, we'll go off to Europe and live happily for the rest of our lives."

"No," she cried, "I consulted a lawyer and he said those letters are proof of adultery and I have no legal right to anything. Absolutely nothing! Do you hear me?"

"He's a fox," said Alejandro. "And you are incredibly stupid for keeping those letters."

"You're the fool for having written them!" she screamed. "Because now they've left us with nothing."

"They're letters of true love. A great love that I still feel for you."

"And I was naive enough to believe you. Maybe you were just after my money."

"Money that you no longer have because of your stupidity!"

She covered her face with both hands and began to cry like a little child. The music returned, the station showed a commercial, and then the program continued.

"We're finished," said Victoria.

"We have to find a solution to this," declared Alejandro.

"No, there is no solution other than finding a job in order to survive."

"Well, I have a great solution," he said with an enigmatic expression. "But I'm not sure if you would agree to it."

"I would do anything to avoid being left penniless," she said. "I was poor once and I know very well what it's like."

The theme song interrupted the scene and the station showed another commercial.

"I can imagine what they're going to do," said the woman.

The old man did not respond because, as usual, he had fallen asleep in front of the television. She got up slowly and went toward the door at the back of the living room, opened it, and entered the bedroom.

The foreman came to meet her and embraced her passionately. The theme song of the soap opera could be heard in the distance, and she thought: "Yes, that is the only way out... She will do to Eduardo the same thing she did to Alvaro, the boyfriend she had before Alejandro... That evil woman..."

Concentrating completely upon guessing the possible outcome of the soap opera, she had not even realized that the foreman had undressed her and eased her onto the sofa, so it was too late for her to react and resist. And feeling completely overcome by his impetuous love, she had only the strength to think: "Yes, Victoria and Alejandro are going to kill Eduardo."

As they surrendered to each other with greater passion than usual, they were unaware that the old man had awakened and was observing them through a secret hole in one of the walls of the living room.

"Tomorrow I'll give them what they deserve," he thought with a certain joy. "They won't escape this alive."

The melody, with even greater shrillness, filled every corner of the mansion.

5

The next afternoon was hot as always. The sun's rays shone on the windows like keys to secret messages.

The woman had replaced the pitcher and was enjoying herself with the foreman in the garden cottage. The old man was sipping his tamarind drink and thinking that it was time to read the comics, and that the soap opera would begin soon, but the irritating voice of the peddler awoke him from his deep meditations.

"Good afternoon, doc!" he said, almost kneeling as if he were going to kiss his hand. For a few pennies I'll do magic tricks for you and tell your fortune."

"Here you are bugging me again! Leave me alone; if you don't I'll call the National Guard on you!"

"You were very powerful. They used to call you 'Iron hand,' right, doc?"

He raised his hand and plucked a flower from the air, offering it to the old man, who just looked at it distrustfully. The peddler put it on the ground next to the rocking chair, and the flower turned into an iguana, which crawled off down the hall and into the house.

"Those times are unforgettable," said the man, sighing. In his eyes gleamed an old, but still burning flame. "Times when I imposed law and order, and imbeciles like you didn't come around trying my patience."

"You used to wipe the town clean of all opposition, isn't that right, doc?"

The peddler vanished. The old man did all he could to hide his surprise. He remained motionless, trying to look bored, his gaze fixed on the garden.

"When I identified the criminals, I ordered that their bodies be brought to me," he said, rubbing his hands and smiling ferociously.

"And they were buried in the garden of the Governor's Palace, right, doc?" said the peddler, appearing behind the rocking chair.

"We used them to fertilize the flower beds. Big, beautiful flowers grew. And, above all, there was no doubt that the troublemakers wouldn't cause any more problems."

"They weren't criminals; they only demanded a minimum wage and schools for their children, right, doctor sir?"

"But they opposed my will. Don't you understand, fool, that at that time I was the one in charge?"

"But see, doc, I have guessed your past," he said, disappearing again and reappearing in front of the old man.

"That's the past," he said impatiently and still incredulous. "I'll give you real money if you tell my future."

"Your future will be decided by Kukulcán[1]," said the peddler.

---

[1]Kukulcán: The feathered serpent, the highest divinity of the ancient Toltecs.

"Kukulcán," he repeated patiently, bending over to reach into a bag and take out a brilliantly colored serpent. "The All-Powerful," he said, as he put it on the man's lap.

"What..., what?" he exclaimed, frightened.

The slow movement of the gleaming reptile's head with its bulging eyes shook him out of his usual state of drowsiness.

"What do you mean?" he screamed, trying desperately to get the snake off without touching it with his trembling hands.

The snake had raised its head level with the old man's and was observing him mysteriously as its fine, pink tongue flicked in and out.

"No, please!" he begged. "Get this thing off me!"

The peddler picked up his bags, turned on his heels and walked away slowly.

"Wait, I beg you!" implored the old man, managing somehow to get his hands into his pockets and pull out a large wad of bills. "Look, all this is yours, and I have more in the house, much more, and many jewels. Take it, it's all yours!"

The peddler went through the gate and disappeared down the road.

Momentarily, a scream broke the silence of the peaceful afternoon.

6

Melancholy music filled the rooms of the enormous house, and a voice announced:

"And now, for you, our kind viewers, the first episode of a new soap opera: 'Claudia's Three Loves,' a tender, dramatic, and unforgettable love story that will conquer your hearts."

(1979-1991)

PHOTOGRAPHER OF DEATH

At the Human Rights Commission, a small office crowded with shelves full of books, volumes of photographs, and walls covered with notes, calendars and messages, an employee was sitting behind a desk reviewing some documents. Seeing two men enter the office hurriedly, he stopped reading and stood up to receive them. One of them came forward to greet him, extending a hand.

"Good morning, we are supposed to meet here with..."

"Are you the reporters?" asked the employee.

"I'm the reporter and he is the photographer," said one of them.

The three greeted each other with warm handshakes.

"Well, as I explained when I spoke with you yesterday," said the reporter, "we need information for a series of articles about the human-rights situation in the country..."

"Please come in and sit down," said the employee.

"Thank you, you are very kind," said the photographer, drying his sweaty forehead with a handkerchief. "Forgive us for coming a little late. The bus we were on got behind schedule; there was a detour because of a protest march..."

"Don't worry, I understand. Nowadays it's impossible to be on time for anything. If it's not one thing it's another."

"That's right, everything is so uncertain," agreed the reporter.

"With regard to the information you need for the articles, I'm willing to cooperate in any way you wish," said the employee, "the only condition being that you not mention my name, that you just call me Teófilo."

"Fine, as you wish," agreed the photographer.

"It's for security reasons," said Teófilo. "You understand."

"We understand perfectly. No problem," said the reporter as he took out a notebook and pencil and prepared to take notes.

"May I take some pictures?" asked the photographer.

"Yes, you may take them of the office, but not of me," explained Teófilo.

"I understand, don't worry."

The man went through the office and took several photos while the reporter was speaking with Teófilo.

"Tell me, what does your work at the Commission consist of?"

"Well, I'm the photographer," answered Teófilo. "Every day I travel 60 kilometers around the city, in search of the victims of the previous night which, I admit, does not require a great deal of effort because dead bodies abound... especially lately, since urban terrorism has increased. Rarely are there less than seven... Once I found forty-six."

"How do you identify them? That is, how do you know where the corpses are?"

"People mark them with cardboard crosses or with branches. I'm guided by the crosses, by the packs of stray dogs digging up bones, or by the vultures flying above the decomposing bodies."

"Is it necessary to move the bodies in order to photograph them?" asked the photographer.

"First they're photographed in the exact position in which they're found," answered Teófilo, "then in parts, especially when they've been tortured... In some cases the whole body can't be photographed because the victim has been decapitated... Sometimes only hands, arms or legs are found..."

"What do you do with the remains?" inquired the reporter.

"We transport them to the nearest cemetery. Sometimes they're buried at the same place where they're discovered, because of the lack of space in the cemeteries."

A woman, visibly upset, entered the office. Teófilo and the reporter stood up.

"I'm looking for my son! Who can help me find him!"

Teófilo went toward her.

"Come in, ma'am. How can I help you?"

"My son disappeared about a week ago," she said hopelessly. "I've gone to all the hospitals and to the Red Cross, but no one gives me any information about him. Please help me!"

"Calm down, ma'am," begged Teófilo. "We will do all we can to find him. The first thing for you to do is to look through these photographs... They are the most recent." He handed her a catalog and pointed to a chair. "Sit down please, and look them over carefully."

Teófilo returned and sat down behind the desk. The photographer accompanied the woman to the corner where the chair was. She sat down and began to look through the catalog under the attentive gaze of the photographer who seemed to want to help her in her search.

"Do you believe that any similarity exists among the victims?" continued the reporter. "That is, in the way they die."

"Curiously, the dead look alike," said Teófilo. "Their faces show identical final expressions, which could well be of pain or of defiance... As if the same one that died yesterday rose today with the light of dawn and was executed again in the darkness... The violence seems to feed on two factions: those who try to exterminate the rebellion, and those who have decided not to die, no matter how much they are killed."

Extremely upset, the woman came toward the desk, pointing to a photograph.

"This is he, sir! This is my son! Look what they've done to him!"

Compassionately, accustomed to that painful scene, the young man stood up and went toward the woman.

"Calm down, ma'am," he said as he observed the photograph carefully for a few seconds. "This body is at the General Cemetery...

Please, ma'am, calm down. We will accompany you if you wish to go and claim it."

"Yes, please, I will thank you with all my heart," she said between sobs. "And somehow I'm going to buy a coffin for my son, because I must bury him as God commands."

2

At the cemetery, as the gravediggers were arriving, the four stood waiting among the headstones. The woman was moaning and Teófilo was consoling her. The reporter was busy recording details in his little notebook. The photographer was examining the surroundings and taking pictures. At that moment, a man who was passing by approached them and, as if he were seized by a terrible desperation, said to them:

"I was told that the body of a woman had been discovered at this cemetery..."

The photographer observed the man with curiosity.

"It's that... my wife disappeared some days ago," he said as if he were crazed. "She is young and pretty... We had just returned from our honeymoon... I've looked for her everywhere... I don't know if she's alive or dead... Have you seen her around here?"

"No, we haven't seen her," said the photographer in a friendly tone. "But you should ask at the cemetery office; maybe they can help you there..."

"What strange times," said the man, "the things that happen... I go through the cemeteries looking for my wife, but... with a certain fear of finding her... Yes, I'm going to ask at the office as you suggest."

The man walked away making strange gestures. "I had to bargain with the gravediggers," Teófilo said to the reporter. "They wanted twenty pesos, but finally they agreed to dig up the body for ten."

"Everyone makes a living any way he can," said the reporter.

The gravediggers finally went down into a grave. The voice of one of them was heard:

"How was the boy dressed? Do you remember the color of his pants or shirt?"

The woman took a few hesitant steps in the direction of the grave and, in a trembling voice, answered:

"Blue pants... And a white shirt... Ah, the shirt was new. I gave it to him two weeks ago, for his eighteenth birthday."

"What material were the pants made of?" asked the other gravedigger.

"I don't remember very well," she said, "maybe Dacron..."

"Did he have any fillings in his teeth?"

"No, none. His teeth were small, white and straight... like his father's... Oh, yes, he did have a gold crown on one of his front teeth."

"Look at this," said one gravedigger, "a piece of white cloth... it looks like part of a shirt..."

The woman approached the grave.

"And look at this jawbone," said the other gravedigger. "It has small, fine teeth and one tooth has a gold crown..."

The woman moved away from the grave, covering her face, horrified. She raised her arms to the sky and shouted:

"Oh my God, why have you allowed him to be killed like a dog!" looking as though she was going to faint.

Teófilo took her by the arm, and said:

"Calm down, ma'am."

"Poor thing! My poor son!" screamed the woman desperately. "It's better not to even touch him anymore. Leave him in peace the way he is."

The woman went off crying like a little child, followed by Teófilo, the reporter, and the photographer.

The gravediggers came out of the grave. One of them carried a bottle of liquor. He tilted the bottle to take a long drink and passed it to the other.

The desperate man who was looking for his wife approached them and asked:

"By any chance, have you seen a woman around here?"

"The only woman I've seen here is death herself," said one of the gravediggers indifferently.

"A horrible, dried-up woman," agreed the other.

"Well, I won't stop searching for my wife until I find her," said the man. "I'll go this way." And he left.

"Who would go around looking for a living person in the cemetery?" said one gravedigger.

"That guy is totally crazy," said the other.

"That's for sure. Not a day goes by that you don't see him walking around the cemetery."

One of the gravediggers brought his hands up to his nose, and said:

"How awful! No matter how much I wash my hands with soap, a strong smell of rotten flesh always remains. Pour some rum on my hands; maybe that will take it away."

"Bah, why should we waste it!" said the other. "Not even the strongest rum erases the smell of the dead!" He took a long drink and passed the bottle to the other gravedigger.

3

At the office of the Human Rights Commission, the employee was reviewing some documents on the desk. In a corner, a young woman was reviewing a collection of photographs. She stood up and went toward the employee.

"It's impossible," she said with disappointment. "I've looked through all the catalogs and I don't see even one photograph with a face resembling my brother's."

"It's really very difficult to recognize them," said the employee, looking at her. "The photographs, in general, don't allow you to make out the faces."

"You can't even tell if they're men or women. They're disfigured... They look like monsters."

"On the other hand, you don't know for sure if your brother is dead. It's possible that he's still alive."

"Possibly, but I doubt it," she said. "He disappeared six months ago..."

"Yes, you're right, that's quite a long time. What did your brother do?"

"He worked days at a warehouse and at night he studied at the university. He was already in his last year of civil engineering studies... He made so many sacrifices in order to go to college."

"It's the only way to get ahead when you're poor."

"My brother was very intelligent... We all had faith that he would become a great man."

"Who knows, maybe he'll turn up."

"He disappeared without even knowing that his wife was pregnant... She's due soon."

"That child is the hope of the future."

At that moment the reporter entered the office, with several newspapers under his arm.

"Good afternoon."

"Good afternoon," said the employee. "How can I help you?"

"Could I speak to Teófilo, please? I'm a reporter. We're working on a series of articles," he said, offering a paper to the employee. "I want to show him the first one that's been published, and get information for the next article in the series."

"Teófilo?" asked the employee.

"Yes, Teófilo, the Commission's photographer," insisted the reporter.

"Teófilo disappeared about five days ago," said the employee. "He's dead."

"Teófilo, dead? It can't be!" said the stunned reporter.

"Yes, just yesterday we found his body."

The employee went and took a picture out of a drawer. He handed it to the reporter who, seeing it, could not hold back the tears; he looked for a chair and sat down and for a moment was silent, with his head bowed and his gaze fixed on the dark floor of the office.

"The Commission itself suffers the same abuses it tries to denounce," said the employee.

"This dreadful picture can't be real! It can't be!" said the reporter, getting up, clutching the photo to his chest, then pointing to it. "Why, just a few days ago I saw that face full of life, dynamic, smiling. It can't be!"

The employee approached the reporter, trying to console him, and said:

"How can I help you, my friend? I'm the new photographer. I'm at your service."

The reporter looked at him enigmatically, and said:

"It's strange, my friend, but your words have the same warm and tranquil tone as Teófilo's, you know?" Then, addressing the young woman, he continued:

"His features show determination, and his gaze, like Teófilo's, is clear and impassive... characteristics which perhaps are necessary to carry out the task of photographing death, and be willing to run the risk of being trapped by it..."

The reporter left the office. The employee took some papers out of a filing cabinet, sat down behind the desk, and began reading them. The young woman continued the search for her brother in the thick catalog of photographs.

THE REPORT

She had come to the headquarters looking for the sergeant, to make a personal report. And now that she was facing him, it was somewhat difficult to accomplish her task, because the man seemed interested in things other than what she was there for. The moment she timidly entered the office, a poorly lighted, dingy room permeated with the strong odors of burned tobacco and cheap after-shave, the man's bulging eyes focused on the young woman's breasts, and for some time it was impossible for him to stop staring, as if those feminine protuberances were strong magnets which trapped his tired eyes.

He asked her to sit down, pointing to an old chair whose dark varnish was worn off the arms and back. Without waiting for her to speak, he began to compliment her figure with a flood of crude adjectives that tumbled out of his wide, misshapen mouth, revealing his dark, broken teeth. More than expressing his thoughts, he seemed to become entangled in a verbal labyrinth as his obscene gaze scrutinized other parts of the girl's body. She remained serene, as if the decision to come to the headquarters had provided her with the patience necessary for precisely that circumstance, and she limited herself to observing the uniformed man as he continued to stubbornly emit those confused words.

In spite of everything, she struggled to put aside the thick verbiage that the sergeant was vomiting, in hopes of finally communicating her message to him. She thought it worth the trouble to try, because it was a situation of which the sergeant certainly should be made aware. Personally, she had resigned herself to reality, and her presence at the headquarters represented the final step toward liberation from certain ghosts of the past, the liberation that had also given her the moral strength necessary to resolutely confront the present, and to face this man who, for the moment, was not showing the least bit of interest in hearing what she had to say.

The sergeant tried to move his chair closer to the desk, with the purpose of approaching the young woman, but his large stomach got in the way, forcing him to get up and walk around the desk with slow, heavy steps. A long, sharp screech rose from the dusty floor, caused by the black boots that protected the man's wide, bulging feet. With great effort, he sat down next to the girl. She had followed the man's clumsy movements with the same tranquil gaze with which she looked at him when she entered the office, a gaze he tried to decipher based on his investigative experience, but he had the sensation of looking into the coldness of an empty mirror, which did not reflect his round, flat face. Then he discovered her light smile, framed by her placid face, illuminated by two enormous and expressive dark eyes. The curved line of her fine red lips made him think that his insistent flirting pleased her, which pushed him to intensify it, make it direct and even a bit more graphic, in order to clearly establish the intention of his words, which were now a direct product of the intense carnal desire that burned in his veins, having invaded him as he became aware of the refreshing youthfulness of the body seated in front of him.

He guessed that the girl's report was certainly another of so many he received every day about robberies, assaults or, in some cases, regarding suspicions of subversion, which did not interest him either, because the investigations section was inundated with that kind of report, to the point of lacking sufficient material and human resources to respond to them. He was very familiar with this situation because he himself, only a few months ago, had directed groups in charge of looking into such reports, true in most cases and at times unfounded suspicions, but which they were obliged to follow up. They would surprise the suspects in their homes, arrest them, take them to headquarters and question them until they made them talk any way they could, peaceful or violent, to determine whether they were guilty of the accusations against them. In many cases, as he himself could attest, the arrests turned into acts of violence, in which members of the group raped the women, especially if they found them alone or with children. They would beat the men and simply shoot them if they tried to escape, as their instructions established. But he no longer needed to get involved in those violent situations. He had been promoted to sergeant because of the "excellent" investigative work he had carried out over the last six months, during which he commanded a unit dedicated to wiping the city clean of subversives. His work had earned him a new uniform, a better salary, an office, and the magnificent opportunity of meeting with women like the one who had come to visit him on this occasion. Now they came to him. And he would not let this one get away; he would win her at all costs, even if he had to make use of all his investigative skills in order to do so.

She, meanwhile, still had the willingness and patience to wait for the sergeant to finally desist from his flirting and listen to her. It had not been easy for her to make the decision to come to the headquarters. She had thought it over and eventually decided it was the best thing to do. Nevertheless, it still made her uncomfortable that the sergeant did not remember her, or that maybe he did recognize her but did not show the least bit of surprise at seeing her there. Or perhaps such details meant little or nothing to him. Even so, it was difficult to accept that he had forgotten her, since his actions and behavior in the past had changed her life radically. She remembered the incident with absolute clarity. The man had come, leading a group, to search the house. Someone had informed the headquarters that a guerrilla hid there, her lover, who at that moment was not at home because he belonged to an insurgent group that was fighting in the mountains. Those who were living there on that occasion, younger brothers and sisters, aunts, and the mother of the girl, denied knowing the man they were looking for. And it was then that the leader of the group locked her in a semi-dark room and raped her. Then they left, leaving her thrown on the bed, with a sharp and bloody pain inside, having stolen from her what she had kept and reserved for her lover, who never returned from the war because, soon after, he died in combat. Within months of being abused, she began to feel ill and the doctor told her she was pregnant. She and her mother discussed her condition at length and concluded that the life she carried inside her was indeed a blessing from God. As the days passed she decided, without being completely sure why, to communicate the fact to the sergeant. And it was for precisely this purpose that she had come.

The man suddenly realized that all the empty talk with which he had barraged the young woman had as yet had no effect. He stood up, went to the window, and observed the horizon through the dusty glass, his back to the girl, gathering his thoughts, trying to devise another angle to return to the attack with greater intensity and efficiency.

She, on the other hand, slowly and silently got up, left the office and then the building, without looking back, gently caressing her abdomen, thinking that, after all, that man did not deserve the happiness of knowing that he was going to be a father, whereas she would be a happy mother. That cruel and bloody war had taken from her the man whom she loved with the fantasy and passion of first love, but the war had also left her a child that now moved within her, to whom she would give all her love in memory of her lover. A faint smile appeared on her face as she imagined the sergeant's look of frustration when he discovered that she was gone.

(1990)

THE TREE OF LIFE

1

One rainy night of thunder and lightning, Casiano surprised Matilde, his fiancee, in bed with Hermógenes, his twin brother.

Instantly the naked Hermógenes grabbed his machete and, like a wild cat, jumped up to attack him.

The twins became entangled in a furious fight of machete blows, curses and blood. Matilde, meanwhile, screaming like crazy, without clothes and without her virginity, ran toward the yard, where she was greeted by thunder and a deadly bolt of lightning which struck her, leaving her lying at the entrance to the house.

In the end Hermógenes mortally wounded Casiano. Through the torrential rain, he dragged the body to a pit near an enormous tree. He also carried Matilde's body there and threw it down next to Casiano's.

The two bodies were left entangled in the tree's thick roots, which protruded from the pit like fearsome serpents.

The roots swallowed them up. Matilde and Casiano came back to life inside the tree, remaining locked in an embrace, united and happy because, when it revived them, the tree erased all traces of hatred from Casiano.

2

Years later, the municipality constructed a park around the huge tree. In honor of its big, beautiful, red flowers, it named the hamlet Pueblo Rojo.

Beneath its shade and to the happy concert of birds, children were baptized, catechism was taught, young people made their First Communion, and couples were joined in matrimony.

On weekends the barber, the shoemaker, and the peddlers would set up shop there.

And every four years the political authorities met under the tree to inaugurate the new mayor.

For the Easter festivals, an altar was constructed in front of the tree's thick trunk. The bishop celebrated mass before the multitude of faithful who made the pilgrimage from neighboring cities and towns.

At the end of the mass, the musicians would liven the carnival with marimbas, guitars, maracas, accordions, drums, flutes, and voices. The people joined the song and dance.

Stands selling delicious traditional food and drink appeared. Children ran to ride the merry-go-round and the "flying chair." The lottery offered incalculable fortunes for five cents.

In her faded tent a toothless gypsy read the palm of a young girl and surprised her with the prediction that she would marry a rich and handsome young man. The girl sighed romantically as the gypsy tucked the dollar between her large breasts.

The circus announced "the greatest spectacle in the world in which a human being turns into a snake." It was a woman disguised as a rattlesnake. But everyone ended up laughing at the clowns' vulgar jokes and the drunken dancers falling all over the "Snake Woman."

The giant tree sheltered the carnival in its shade. It provided a cool breeze and the warbling of orioles and mockingbirds. Its flowers descended to the ground to form a red carpet on which young and old would dance until night fell.

3

Civil war seized the country. The government undertook the task of wiping the area clean of insurgents.

One mild summer afternoon the troops arrived in Pueblo Rojo. Some of the inhabitants managed to flee to the mountains. When they returned to the town, it had been reduced to rubble. They dug a large pit in the plaza near the tree and buried the dead.

At nightfall the enormous roots swallowed them up and they came back to life inside the tree. Elderly people, women and children, soldiers and rebels, even the town priest, met their relatives, friends and enemies, to live happily together within the majestic and benevolent tree.

(1981)

THE FACES OF XIPOTEC

1

The Military Base Market, or the "Burned Base Market," as some Salvadorans prefer to call it, occupies the half-acre of land where the Central Headquarters of the Army formerly stood. The origin of the fire is unknown, but what is certain is that it completely destroyed the military base. Later the area was paved and small businesses that sold clothing, shoes and crafts were established there.

It was precisely in this place that a soda shop, well-known for the excellent quality of its drinks, was located. Since I was already in the neighborhood, I thought it was a good time to check out its reputation for myself, and at the same time quench the thirst brought on by the burning midday sun.

So I entered the market and began to walk through the labyrinth of unending hallways and lines of stores saturated with merchandise, odors, voices, shouts and music. I walked among women, men and children, all carrying packages, moving busily in all directions. Suddenly I noticed the sign for "The Face," hanging above the entrance to a narrow refreshment stand situated between a shoe store and a clothing shop.

Its interior was full of pots of different sizes and glasses which a woman hurried to wash as she hummed along with the romantic song coming from a radio hidden in a corner. On the colorless walls hung calendars showing religious images and exotic landscapes, all of them surrounding a faded reproduction of a saint difficult to identify at first glance. On a small table in the back stood a statue of Saint Martin of Porres, illuminated by a candle next to a vase full of wax flowers. Between the saint and the landscapes was a small painting in which a dark-green color predominated.

I asked the woman if she would let me have a closer look at the picture and she, alarmed at my request or perhaps distrustful, refused to let me in, but did hold the candle up to the painting.

"It's a face," she said dryly, as she held the light up to it.

"The face of the devil!" I exclaimed, without intending to.

She moved the light away. I inquired whether she was the owner of the business and, covering her bruised cheek with her hand, she said that the owner had suffered an accident, that he was hospitalized, and that he would be back next week.

I paid for the drink and headed toward the exit to the market. Before I crossed to another hallway, I looked back at the shop and my eyes met those of the woman, who was watching me with some curiosity, making strange expressions with her round, hairy, mistreated face. Her smile revealed many missing teeth.

I went out to the street, fighting the heat and my thirst. The well-known drinks were not all that great after all. The memory of the macabre image made me nauseous. Luckily, when I boarded the bus to go home, I was feeling better and I promised myself that I would never return to that place.

Nevertheless, a week later, inexplicably, I found myself at "The Face" again. On this occasion, a heavy woman wearing a ridiculously short bright red dress, waited on me. She wore a gold chain around her fat, sweaty neck. A floral handkerchief barely covered her thick, messy, black curly hair.

"What flavor can I get you?" she asked, smiling, revealing crooked, yellow teeth with several gold crowns. "The horchata is delicious."

I asked for a drink, what flavor I don't remember, because I wasn't there so much to calm my thirst as to satisfy my curiosity to see the frightful painting again.

Part of my interest in the work possibly was related to my fondness for watercolors, a technique I learned by reading painting manuals. I don't consider myself a professional artist, but from time to time I paint a landscape, a still life, or a vase of flowers. Especially flowers, since that is what attracts people the most. My works are at my mother's store, an odd art gallery in which watercolors are displayed next to articles of basic necessity such as rice, corn and beans; bread, cheese and cream; fruit, eggs, candy, sodas and cigarettes. It occurred to my mother to use them to decorate the store, but as time went by they aroused a certain degree of interest among her customers and became another object of consumption. The proceeds from these sales complemented my austere salary as a public school teacher.

It was a pity that the customers couldn't examine my paintings closely because, due to the crime and violence which had broken out as a result of the armed conflict in the country, access to the inside of the store was prohibited to them. The entrance was blocked with thick iron bars that gave the gloomy appearance of a prison. This became the norm for all the businesses in the city.

When I asked to talk to the owner, a short old man with quick eyes appeared from the back of the small establishment. Immediately, as if he knew the purpose of my visit, he claimed that he didn't know the origin of the painting and he emphasized that it was there when he acquired the business. He added that he wouldn't sell the painting either, because it was so encrusted in the wall that to get it off it would be necessary to destroy the wall, and that was prohibited. Nevertheless, without my asking him, and with apparent pleasure, he projected candlelight onto the painting, at the same time breaking out in raucous laughter, which was joined by laughter and incoherent words from the woman. In a corner of the painting I was able to make out the signature of the artist, Xipotec, in yellow letters.

I left the market and without wasting any time I went to the home of the prior owner of the business who, according to the old man, lived in Colonia Manzano. I got on the bus and fifteen minutes later I got off near the Presidential House. To save time I decided to ask a person I stopped on the street for directions.

"Six blocks to the left and four to the right," the man said, covering his mouth as he spoke, as if he were telling me a secret or perhaps hiding his toothless mouth.

I followed his instructions and a short time later I was at the same bus stop where I had just gotten off. This time I walked six blocks to the right and four to the left. I found Las Cruces street and looked for house number six. Reaching it, I knocked on the door with great insistence. A shirtless boy appeared from the house next door.

"That entrance is sealed off," he said. "What do you need?"

"I'm looking for Sófocles. Does he live here?"

"Come in this way," he said, walking ahead of me through narrow hallways between gardens, an atmosphere permeated with the perfume of flowers and the strong odors of food, smoke, gas, alcohol and feces. We ended up in front of a man who was resting in a hammock.

"Don Sofo, this man is here to see you," said the shirtless boy. But the man didn't respond. The boy shook the hammock:

"Don Sofo, wake up, someone's here to see you."

He woke up with a start, as if he had been having a horrible nightmare. He invited me to sit down and offered me a fresh fruit drink in a glass of the same kind and color as those used in "The Face." He looked so much like the quick-eyed man at the market that I couldn't help but comment.

"We're twins," he said calmly, getting up. "My brother looks younger than I do because he takes better care of himself."

I got right to the point and asked him about the painting. A strange look came over his face, and then he admitted that it was a gift from Xipotec. Then immediately he warned me that it was impossible for him to say anything further about the matter, and as he said this he looked around, as if he feared he was being watched. Then he turned his back on me, got into the hammock and began drinking in silence, looking at me out of the corner of his eye.

At the end of the hallway there was a room with an open door. Inside I discovered a large painting of a greenish face with bulging eyes which appeared to give off flames. Observing the work of art and feeling the energy it projected toward me, I vowed not to leave the place until I found out where the painter was. My silence and stubborn presence demonstrated my determination; I just hoped the old man would understand that.

"He lives in Panchimalco," he finally said, without looking at me.

"Thank you, you're very kind," I responded, and I left.

2

The next day I found myself at the bus station waiting for the bus that would take me to the indigenous town of Panchimalco. The vehicle appeared and was immediately boarded by a variety of passengers, including workers, peasants, children and women carrying bags and baskets. It left the station and entered the street to begin the trip under the burning sun which filled the inside of the old bus with a hot vapor.

Trying to ignore the heat, I began reading the newspaper, which was full of the usual reports of violence: armed confrontations and arrests; disappearances, bombings and demonstrations; massacres in the interior of the country. The Human Rights Commission reported hair-raising statistics: between 254 and 300 victims of the civil war each week, including the disappeared, the tortured, and the dead.

In its slow course, the bus had pulled away from the crowded traffic of the city and was now travelling through the outlying areas. It took the steep highway toward Los Planes de Renderos, which is located on a mountaintop, and passed elevated points from which I could see the busy city of San Salvador, whose tentacles extended to the slopes of mountains and volcanoes. Once in Los Planes de Renderos, the bus turned and began to descend toward the village of Panchimalco. It travelled along a dusty road which soon became a stone street. It proceeded slowly along several streets of the old village and stopped in a quadrangle that appeared to be the central plaza.

All the passengers, including the driver, got out of the bus and disappeared down the streets of the town in a matter of minutes. We had finally arrived in Panchimalco, and I stepped out into the street. The dazzling white color and attractive colonial architecture of the church immediately caught my eye. The Devil's Door, an enormous opening formed by two gigantic rocks on the mountain peak behind the town, complemented the imposing landscape.

Panchimalco is a Pre-Columbian city founded by Toltecs, who possibly emigrated to this region after the dissolution of their empire in Tabasco, Mexico, bringing with them their culture and their highest divinity, Kukulcán, "the God of the feathered serpent." Their eventual descendants, the Pipil race, populated most of El Salvador, formerly known as Cuscatlán or "land of jewels."

According to some historians, Panchimalco is a place of refuge, since it was the area in which the Cuscatlecans regrouped as a last alternative of defense against the sophisticated invasion of the Spaniards in the 16th century. From there comes the name which one of the mountains surrounding the city received, Chulo, or Chulu, which means "place of the fugitive."

The name Panchimalco derives from the Nahuatl words pan, pant and panti: flags; chimal: shield; and co: place and means "place of shields and flags." According to the Book of Government of Santa Cruz Parish of Panchimalco, construction of the beautiful church began in April of 1543, by the Indians residing in the village under the direction of Spanish priests, and was finished in April of 1730. The first baptismal certificate was written in 1655. From the beginning of its construction, the temple was an important symbol of the Catholic Church and a principal center during the intense campaign to convert to Christianity the Indians who occupied the region, the Panchos, whose direct descendants still reside in Panchimalco.

Suddenly I felt the urge to commend myself to God, and I walked toward the church. I stopped in the entrance to observe the figures of the saints, eight in all, set in niches, perhaps to welcome the faithful or to protect the entry to the temple and detain the evil spirits which, according to some of the local residents, descend into the town at midnight from the Devil's Door.

I entered the church and remained there a long time, appreciating its hot, desolate interior. I admired the statues of the saints, their gazes crystallized in strange expressions, and the decorated wooden altars, especially that of San Francisco. The ancient, dark paintings suddenly reminded me of the horrible faces in Xipotec's pictures, which again took over my thoughts and pushed me to leave the sanctuary.

I walked down a wide stone street away from the church. I knocked on the door of a house to ask about the painter named Xipotec. A woman came out and told me to wait. She then disappeared behind a curtain and immediately returned holding a greenish image which showed a horrible face with eyes that seemed to leap right out of the painting.

"Yes, I'm familiar with those paintings," I exclaimed, among other things. "I want to see the painter."

The old woman laughed loudly and slammed the door, shouting to me from inside that I should go to the house at the end of the path, to my right.

I truly desired to find the painter. His works had awakened in me an obsession difficult to explain. I was determined to find out what method he used to achieve those faces with such mastery of expression and detail. On the other hand, his imagination intrigued me. What motivated him to paint those horrendous images? What were the concepts on which that horror was based?

It was obvious that Xipotec's compositions and mine had nothing in common. But that was precisely what attracted me to them. I was convinced that I could learn a great deal from this artist from Panchimalco. I felt that those images were closer to reality, to the drama that is life, and that Xipotec knew the technique and the artistic concepts to create them in painting.

Oddly, at that moment I was again gripped by an urge to abandon my search, to return to the city and leave that strange place as soon as possible. Something seemed to be telling me that there was still time to desist from my undertaking.

But stronger than my will was the overwhelming curiosity that had taken hold of me: the desire to meet the artist of those demonic faces which seemed to stupefy everyone who saw them. I myself, possibly, was bewitched by the hypnotism that emanated from the diabolical eyes of those dark images.

I was going toward the dwelling the old woman had indicated, observing that the doors and windows of the small homes were opening and closing. It was then that I noticed that something or someone was coming toward me on the path. It looked like a shape wrapped in a fiery-red robe. I immediately got out of the way and let it pass.

"Curiosity is the beginning and end of secrets," said the deep voice that came from the form as it passed by me, giving off flames and charring even the rocks along its way. It moved away, leaving smoke and ash behind.

A confused sensation invaded me, and for a few seconds I wasn't sure if I was awake or dreaming. The burning rays of the sun marked the shadows of objects on the ground with such intensity that they looked as if they were painted a thick, bright, black color, like tar.

At the end of the path I saw an adobe house, on the door of which hung a handmade sign that read "The Face."

"What a coincidence that in such a remote town there's a store with the same name as the one in the Burned Base Market," I thought, surprised, not realizing that I was talking aloud to myself.

When I entered the small establishment, I tripped on something that made me stumble into the room. Suddenly I was gripped by the dark premonition that something fatal was waiting for me, something I would regret for the rest of my life.

The walls of the store were covered with greenish paintings of faces with indecipherable expressions. To my astonishment, there was the woman with the scratched face and the missing teeth, next to the heavy woman with the ridiculously short, bright-red dress. The old man with the small quick eyes was sitting in a corner, petrified, as if he hadn't moved from there in an eternity. In the other corner there hung a hammock whose slow back-and-forth movement produced a squeaking sound that put my nerves on edge. It was Sófocles, the twin brother, resting in the hammock as he drank from a glass.

"What can I get you?" asked the heavy woman, apparently undisturbed by my visit, as if they had been expecting me.

This time I didn't ask for a drink, but rather to see the painter.

"I want to talk to Xipotec!" I begged, in a voice I had never heard before.

No one paid any attention to me. Sófocles' brother got up from his chair and went to close the door of a room from which strange noises were beginning to come, like those of an imprisoned animal struggling to escape.

"What flavor would you like?" asked the woman as she wiped her sweaty face with a yellow handkerchief.

The noises from the room turned into loud screams and moans. The sweaty woman and one of the twins went toward the room. She pulled the door and, entering, closed it immediately. The screams became howls and got more and more intense, mixing with the curses of the woman and the old man.

"What's going on in there? Where is the painter?" I asked the woman who remained behind the counter and continued stirring the drinks, paying no attention whatsoever to my pleas, nor showing the least bit of uneasiness about the noise in the other room.

But then the voices, screams and howls became an intolerable uproar, and were followed by the sounds of something or someone hitting the walls and objects falling to the floor and breaking. It finally reached the point that the woman in front of me stopped smiling and began to show signs of concern; now she too wanted to find out what was happening. She went toward the room and slowly opened the door a crack. As soon as she stuck her head in she disappeared abruptly, as if the room had swallowed her up, and she let out a scream of pain.

The old man in the hammock, meanwhile, continued to observe me with his cold gaze, immutable in the face of my desperation and the disturbance in the room.

"What's going on in there?" I shouted, determined this time to go into that chamber whose interior perhaps would be hell itself.

I breathed as deeply as I could to fill my lungs with oxygen and courage. I threw open the counter's gate and went through it. I gained momentum and began to run toward the room, ready to hurl myself against the door and knock it down if necessary. But, to my surprise, the door opened seconds before I made contact with it.

I found myself in the center of a room dimly illuminated by a candle. I was able to see then that the two women and Sófocles' brother were standing around a bed, on which someone was writhing and moaning.

"That's Xipotec," said the twin. "The painter."

"He's my son," affirmed the heavy woman as she applied a damp cloth to the sick man's forehead. His eyes were bulging and had taken on an intense red color. His purple tongue was hanging out. His hair was disheveled.

"What sort of illness does he have?" I asked, perplexed.

"We don't know what it is," said the mother. "He has these convulsions very often."

"I'm so very sorry," I said, suddenly seized by grief and sadness at the pain of the boy and his family. "And when did he start having these attacks?"

"Since they took him prisoner and tortured him. According to him, they used such extreme tortures that it's a miracle of God that he's not dead. He paints those pictures to erase from his mind the face of the one who made him suffer."

"He swears that the prison where they held him was hell, and that his torturer was the devil himself," said the woman with the scratched face. "When he gets these attacks, he gets wild and can destroy everything he finds. He even harms us, his own family."

"When his illness calms down, then he paints. It's the only thing that makes him forget the intense pain they subjected him to," said Sófocles, entering the room. He added, "We protect him so they won't capture him again. That's why we didn't want to give you any information. We thought you were looking for him to hurt him."

"No, for God's sake," I said. "I just wanted to meet the painter. I never imagined that he had experienced such torment. I never thought that in order to paint that way the artist would have to suffer so much."

I went out of the room and left the house, filled with great consternation and sadness. The screams of pain could be heard out in the street.

3

I visited the artist on countless occasions and eventually we managed to form a deep friendship. I learned from him the secrets of his technique and I succeeded in painting with the same mastery.

Some time later, unable to recover from the emotional shock of the torture, he died, weakened by intense convulsions.

Since then I have dedicated myself to painting faces. And even though many years have gone by since his death, time has been unable to erase from my memory Xipotec's painful drama, which has been the greatest influence on my own painting.

(1979 - 1995)

LAURA'S AFFLICTION

1

When she awoke it was eight o'clock in the morning, time to be at work, and she was still at home.

"Today they'll fire me for sure," she thought fearfully, remembering that last month, when her husband was killed, the boss had reproached her with humiliating shouts in front of all the employees because she missed two days of work for the wake and burial. She surely would have been dismissed then, had she not permitted the owner of the store to abuse her sexually the time he called her to the office to talk about a supposed raise, which she never received. Given the state of civil war the country was in, it was difficult if not impossible to get a job, even for a miserable salary like the store paid, and she had to take care of her two fatherless children.

Laura had had nightmares about fire and blood. She had dreamed that, with her husband, she was planting bombs in the city and kidnapping a businessman.

While she was getting dressed she heard on the radio that several buildings in San Salvador had been blown up the night before.

She went out to the street to take the bus in the usual place. As she stood in the aisle of the crowded bus, surrounded by students in white uniforms, she saw a man's picture under the headline "Kidnapped" on the front page of the newspaper that a passenger seated in front of her was reading.

"Pure coincidence," she said to herself, astonished by the dramatic similarity between the news on the radio, the newspaper, and her nightmare. The photograph showed the same elderly, bald man that they had kidnapped at gunpoint.

The coincidences were horrifying her now. Nevertheless, the nightmare left her with a strange feeling of joy because it had allowed her to be near her beloved, deceased husband.

She got off the bus and crossed the street to go to the store, which was located in the center of the city. She became filled with horror again when, on passing in front of the smoking rubble of what used to be a building, she recognized the place. In the dream, she herself had dynamited it.

"Pure coincidence," she thought again, trying to convince herself that everything was only a dream that strangely coincided with reality.

That had to be it! There was no other explanation. The proof was that in the dream she was mortally wounded, but now she was alive.

"The coincidences end here," she thought, finally convinced.

Absorbed in her pondering, she was walking along without realizing that she had joined the ranks of a protest march, which suddenly was attacked by machine-gun fire and turned into a battle between demonstrators and police.

The marchers scattered. Several dead bodies were left lying in the street. She was one of them.

2

She awoke with a start. She touched her body anxiously and looked around. She wanted to be sure she was alive. Then immediately she looked at the bed, experiencing a great sense of relief when she saw that her husband was sleeping soundly next to her.

(1982)

THE RIVER GODDESS

One of my favorite pastimes was to sit on the bank of the river and contemplate the sky as the sun sank into the wet surface of the majestic Lempa.

I remember the times when, with my father, I would travel the dusty roads on the way home from the school where he taught and I was a student. He would tell stories and legends about this river, the spirit of the village, the provider of food, mystery, and fantasy.

One afternoon, among the rocks along the shore, we saw some alligators fighting over a kill. They dealt each other great blows with their tails and their sharp teeth shone in their enormous jaws.

The shower of stones we hurled at them, and our shouts, frightened them. One by one they went off into the water. When they had gone, we went to the place where they had been and looked in the mud, hoping to find what they had been fighting over.

"It's Lempa! It's Lempa, the goddess of the river!" exclaimed my father with great surprise as he picked up a small statue.

The branches of several trees were bending down as if to drink from the river. We pulled off several of their large leaves to clean the statue. We were then able to appreciate the face, the long hair, the nude bust. The rest of the body had an alligator's feet and tail.

We returned to the road which led home.

"The legend," said my father, carrying the idol under his arm, "says that the goddess protects those who live near the river. That everyone who sees this statue is entitled to a wish which can be requested only when one is in danger of dying."

"And do you believe it, Papá?" I remember having asked.

"It's a Mayan legend. They say that the goddess lives in the depths among fish and alligators, that this statue absolutely cannot be possessed by anyone."

"Then we must throw it back into the river!" I said fearfully. "Before something bad happens to us."

"Don't worry, son. Those are just stories that people tell."

Suddenly we heard strange noises. The alligators were running through the bushes as if they were chasing us, their thrashing tails striking the trees. The river seemed to have risen; it was raging, as if threatening to overflow its banks and flood the village. We hurried and arrived home just as the sun was beginning to set.

"Where did you find that?" asked my mother, who recognized the idol immediately. "Get it out of here. I don't want it in my house. A curse could fall on us."

"Pure superstition," declared my father. "I'm going to donate it to the National Museum. It's an object of great archeological value, original and beautiful, worthy of being in a museum and not to be left in the depths of the river."

She disagreed with his decision but did not try to dissuade him. He left the idol on a chair in a dark corner of the living room.

As we were having supper, my father told us how pleased he was with the growing attendance of children at school despite the violent civil war the country was experiencing. When we finished eating, my mother went into the kitchen, my father began reading, and I concentrated my attention on my homework.

Bedtime came, but the legend of the goddess Lempa obsessed me. I tossed and turned in my bed. I felt chills when I thought about the dark, half-woman, half-reptile idol.

Near midnight my nerves were put on edge by a noise which sounded as if the door were being beaten down. I got up and looked out the window toward the patio. There was a full moon. I saw several alligators lurking outside the house.

I was finally able to fall asleep in the early hours of the morning, when the roosters were beginning to crow.

That morning I woke up with a cold. My father left for school. I stayed home all day in my mother's care.

About five o'clock in the afternoon I heard a scream, followed immediately by another, and I jumped up in alarm. I ran outside to see what was happening.

I found my mother crying, her arms in the air. When she saw me, she screamed desperately:

"Your father has been killed!"

"Who killed him?" I screamed, running toward her open arms.

Gripping the hands of the teacher who had come with several people from town to give us the dreadful news, I begged to know:

"Who killed my father?"

"This afternoon some men arrived at school," he said. "They were looking for your father to arrest him."

"Arrest him for what? He never harmed anyone!"

"They said that they did not know why, but that they had strict orders to capture him. He resisted. He tried to escape, but they shot him in the back and he fell mortally wounded; then they took his body away with them."

"I followed them without their seeing me," said a student. "They put his body in a bag and threw it into the river. The alligators ate it."

"I can't understand why they came to arrest him," said the teacher. "Your father was an exemplary man because of his love for others. If that is a crime, then the priest and all the good people of this town are criminals, too."

My mother clung to me, crying bitterly. I consoled her as I tried uselessly to contain my own sobs. I felt that something strange, something I never knew before, had entered my heart. Life later revealed to me that it was "hatred."

Days, weeks, months went by. Time proved that destiny is irreversible, that the deepest sorrow does not bring back even the best loved of our dead.

My mother lost her mind. She would call to my father day and night, kissing his photograph and cursing the goddess Lempa. Days later she lost her ability to speak.

Every night several alligators would gather outside our house. They made strange sounds and pushed at the door. Even during the day it was common to see one or more of them dozing in the yard. Once, I don't know how, one got into the house. We found it hiding under my mother's bed and were able to scare it out of the house with a burning candle.

One afternoon when I was outside feeding the chickens, I saw my mother leave the house with the statue of the goddess Lempa in her hands. From the bank she threw the idol down onto the rocks. At night the river rose and pulled the statue down to its depths.

On a rainy morning when the river was beginning to overflow its banks, my mother took off running, screaming things that made no sense. A dark foreboding flashed like lightning in my brain, pushing me to go after her, but it was too late. She had thrown herself into the water. When I tried to rescue her she had already been devoured by the hungry alligators.

From that moment on, my attraction for the river grew in a sick way. Simply sitting on a rock on the bank gave me strange pleasure, not to watch the sunset as before, but to observe the alligators closely as they slid through the weeds and submerged themselves in the strongest current.

One time, the monotonous sound of the flowing water made me fall into a deep sleep there on the rocks. Suddenly, I was awakened violently by a searing pain as I felt that my leg was being torn off.

One alligator was pulling my body and another had me trapped by my arm. I felt my head inside those powerful jaws that were surely going to decapitate me.

As I agonized, being torn into pieces, I remembered my father telling me about the legend of the goddess Lempa. I cried to her that I did not want to die!

A warm wind blew through my body. I felt myself coming back to life.

The reptiles abandoned their ferocity. Swimming in circles in the water, they seemed to invite me to join them, to submerge my body, now propelled by my powerful tail. Then I recognized my parents: two alligators who seemed to have been waiting for me in the river forever.

(1980)

"The rosemary's[2] flowers
Isabel child
today are blue
tomorrow
they will be honey."

Luis de Góngora y Argote.

THE SPIRIT OF THINGS

1

Miguel Angel was approaching his twentieth birthday. "You were born on a sunny day of blue skies," his mother had said more than once, but such words meant little or nothing to him. It was all the same to him to have been born on a cloudy day or a starry night; there was no difference between day and night. He was blind from birth.

His perception of the world depended in part upon touch and, in greater part, upon hearing. "Everything has a special sound," he would say to his inseparable mother. "Especially in silence, objects give off energy, as if they are breathing. That is when I identify them. The same thing happens with people."

He lived with his mother in Barrio San Jacinto, on Tenth Street, near a bus stop. "There goes the number 11," he would say when he heard the bus go by. At first she would hurry to the door to observe with great admiration, perhaps with astonishment, the passengers who actually were getting in and out of the very bus referred to by her son.

Miguel Angel was familiar with all the objects in the house to the point of knowing with amazing accuracy the location of each one of them. His favorite was the radio, an old model, according to his mother's description, on a table in the corner of the living room. Several slightly faded framed photographs hung on the walls. One showed the face of a man with a large moustache and bulging eyes. Another, a woman of white complexion with a round hairdo and a long dress with a low neckline.

"They are your grandparents," his mother had told him. "He, an army man, carouser and womanizer. She, self-sacrificing and reserved, but of strong character. When she found out that your grandfather was cheating on her, she left him once and for all, in spite of being pregnant, within two months of giving birth to me."

Like all objects, those photographs emitted, for Miguel Angel, a certain sensation which he translated to his mother with the following words:

"My grandfather gives off a nauseating odor, a mixture of gunpowder, rum and vomit. I hear him cry and scream, as if he were being tortured in hell. My grandmother, on the other hand, radiates a perfume of roses. She laughs and sings surrounded by children, as if she were in paradise."

2

On Sundays the radio of the house was tuned to YSAX, the station which broadcast the mass celebrated by Monsignor Romero, Archbishop of San Salvador, from the Metropolitan Cathedral.

Mother and son would sit in the corner of the living room and listen in silence to the Sunday sermon which Monsignor Romero would link to the tragic and violent times their country was experiencing. That voice, energetic and implacable, had sparked the admiration and interest of Miguel Angel for the bishop, especially when he preached: "People also are oppressed when they are kept in the darkness of ignorance. One who doesn't know is like one who doesn't see. Blessed are those who do not see, and those who thirst for justice, because theirs will be the kingdom of light and justice."

"What is Monsignor like, Mamá? Tall? Short?"

"Of medium height, son. And calm and cheerful."

"How strange, because when I hear his voice, I imagine a tall, strong man with great personal magnetism."

"They say that he is shy and reserved, but that when he enters the pulpit he becomes a great preacher, as if God were illuminating him."

"I would love to meet him."

"One of these days we will go to the cathedral for Mass," promised the mother. "Some day when not too many people attend. Because sometimes you can't even get inside the door of the church. Everyone wants to see Monsignor and touch even the hem of his robes."

3

Word spread through the neighborhood that the Archbishop of San Salvador was going to visit the area. Miguel Angel's mother wasted no time in finding out all the details and promised her son that his wish would be fulfilled.

The afternoon of the Archbishop's visit, mother and son waited on the side of the dusty stone street where the prelate was to pass. Others waited along with them: half-naked, dirty, big-bellied children, women, elderly people in rags, and drunken men lying along the side of the street.

"Here comes Monsignor!" they shouted.

A cloud of dust and a great tumult accompanied him. Women held up their children and offered them to Monsignor and he, not minding the filth, took them in his arms.

Miguel Angel's mother took him by the hand and both of them went to stand in the middle of the street. The tumultuous throng approached them and, unable to contain its momentum, caught them up, causing the boy to fall flat on his face in the dust, and his mother on top of him.

"You're going to kill my son!" she exclaimed. "Please, help me get him up!"

Her desperate shouts captured the attention of the people and for a moment the crowd calmed down and fell silent.

The mother took the boy by the arm as another person came forward to help her. Once on her feet she realized that the one helping her was the bishop, who was greeting her with a smile.

"Monsignor!" she said excitedly. "This is my son. He is blind from birth, but he wanted to meet you in person."

"What is your name?" the prelate asked, grasping one of the boy's hands.

"Miguel Angel, Monsignor," he answered, taking the bishop's hand and passing it softly over his dry but open eyes.

The cleric understood the blind boy's desire and put his arms around him, hugging him warmly.

"I don't perform miracles, young man, not by any means," he said in a humble voice.

"Don't worry, Monsignor," said Miguel Angel. "I don't see things but I perceive their spirit."

"A very special gift," declared Monsignor. "There are those who look but do not see. Those who touch but do not feel. In this sense, all of us suffer from a certain blindness."

Then he took something from his pocket and put it in the hands of the blind boy. It was his own rosary.

The mother tried to kneel to kiss his hand, but Monsignor asked her not to and helped her up from the dusty road.

"You have a very intelligent son. Give thanks to God."

The crowd began to shout again. Pushed along by the momentum of the hubbub and the multitude of men, women and children, the bishop continued on his way.

Mother and son remained behind in the middle of the street. He, smiling and hugging the rosary to his chest. She, watching the crowded throng of ragged people moving away, enveloped in the cloud of dust which transported it through the hovels of the neighborhood.

4

Monsignor Oscar Arnulfo Romero y Galdámez, Archbishop of San Salvador, was assassinated by a gunshot on Monday, March 24, 1980 at 6:30 in the afternoon while officiating at a funeral mass in Divine Providence Chapel in the capital.

According to statements gathered in the emergency room of the Salvadoran Polyclinic where his body was taken, a shot rang out like a "bomb blast" at the precise moment when he was raising the chalice for the consecration of the wine. Monsignor collapsed at the feet of a crucifix.

In the emergency room and halls of the Polyclinic there was a great crowd of priests, religious and lay people, and some relatives of Monsignor, whose body lay lifeless, still in its priestly vestments, showing a small bullet hole precisely alongside the heart.

In his final Sunday homily, Monsignor Romero had said: "I would like to make a special appeal to the men of the army and specifically to the bases of the National Guard, the police, and the military: Brothers, you are our own people; you are killing your own peasant brothers and sisters; and an order given by a man, the law of God, which says DO NOT KILL, must prevail. No soldier is compelled to obey an order contrary to the law of God. No one need comply with an immoral law. It is time for you to regain your conscience and obey your conscience and not the order of sin. The church, defender of God-given rights, of God's law, of human and personal dignity, cannot remain silent in the face of such abomination. We want the government to take seriously the fact that reforms which come stained with so much blood are useless. In the name of God, then, and in the name of this suffering people whose laments rise to Heaven more tumultuously each day, I beg you, I implore you, I order you in the name of God: Stop the repression!"

5

In memory of Monsignor Romero, Miguel Angel's mother made a small altar in a corner of their living room. On a little table, in front of a wall with his photograph, she put the treasured rosary, two candelabras with candles, and a vase with wax flowers, which were replaced with fresh flowers on holidays and especially on the anniversary of his death.

Miguel Angel assured his devoted mother that Monsignor Romero had not died.

"I know that you say that to comfort me," she would reply. "And I thank you."

But the blind boy insisted that he was serious and, at the least expected moments, he would shout with great excitement:

"You see, Mamá, there goes Monsignor Romero! There he goes!"

His mother would run to the door and with her anxious gaze would search the street in all directions. At times she saw a child, at times a bird, but inexplicably she always experienced a deep inner joy, so much so that she would declare:

"You're right, my son; Monsignor Romero has not died!"

(1985)

THE GARDEN OF GUCUMATZ

1

They broke down the door with a great crash and burst into the house. The leader took up his position in the center of the living room and shouted:

"Nobody move or I'll shoot!" as he held his revolver with both hands, his arms stretched forward and his body slowly turning to aim the gun in all directions. The others went through the remaining rooms, searching them.

The leader went out to the garden and immediately the birds in their cages became frightened; black, red and yellow butterflies took flight and went to land on the head of an imposing statue of Gucumatz[3], whose gaze of millenarian stone seemed to watch over the tranquility of the garden.

After circling the fountain, the leader examined the bushes, moving them with the barrel of his gun, and then he approached the pool in which the water rippled like an elastic mirror. Seeing his reflection, he could not contain his astonishment. "Son of a bitch, I didn't think I was so ugly," he thought as he caressed the dark, bulging mole next to his nose. He spit into the fountain scornfully. His reflection broke into fragments, like a broken mirror.

The others came out to the garden, and one of them said:

"There's no one here. This place is more lonely than a cemetery."

---

[3]According to the Popul Vuh, Gucumatz is one of the creators of the universe.

Suddenly the chief pointed his weapon toward the end of the corridor and said:

"There he is; now be very careful, be alert, don't trust him."

They couldn't see anything, but they automatically obeyed his orders and aimed their weapons in the direction indicated by the revolver of the chief, who was slowly approaching a hammock which hung from two pillars in the hall.

The body of an elderly man, completely motionless, mouth open and eyes closed, occupied the hammock.

"I think this guy is dead," said one man, examining him cautiously.

"It looks that way," agreed the leader.

A third man pushed the hammock but the old man still did not move.

"This is all we needed," he said, "to find a dead man."

They lowered their arms and assumed a resting position. One of them sank into an armchair while another, putting his weapon away in its holster, went to close the door and began to look through the house absent-mindedly. The chief remained standing in front of the old man, observing him closely, finding no sign of life in him.

"And this is the fearsome guerrilla they told us so much about? The one they warned us to be very careful with because of how dangerous he was?" asked the one who was sitting comfortably in the armchair. "This old man couldn't harm a fly! He doesn't even move!"

"Maybe they gave us the wrong address," said the leader.

"Let's wait. Maybe the one we're looking for lives here and will be back soon. Then we'll get him."

"Okay," agreed the chief. "Let's rest while we wait. If we go back to Headquarters now, for sure they'll send us to pick up another one. There are so many on the list."

The two men were waiting a short distance from the hammock. They felt extremely tired due to the many missions they carried out every day, which were now becoming a matter of routine. Yesterday afternoon's was still fresh in their memories:

They had broken into a house in a poor neighborhood of the city in order to apprehend a man accused of cooperating with the guerrillas. At that moment he was in the dining room talking with his wife, waiting for their daughter so they could have supper together as was their custom.

Moments after the men entered the house, the daughter arrived and, seeing them, became frightened and thought about fleeing, but the anxiety that darkened her parents' faces made her stay.

"And who is this?" asked the leader.

"My daughter," responded the father, while two men held him and another tied his hands.

"Ha, she just came from a demonstration!" said one of the men.

"No, sir, she was at school!" cried the mother. "Can't you see her uniform?"

"Take off your clothes!" the leader ordered the girl. "We must see if you're carrying weapons."

The schoolgirl stood motionless and silent. The man approached her and struck her in the face, a blow which was also felt by her parents and wounded their faces. Then he tore off the white, starched blouse of her neat school uniform.

The mother tried to say something but the words became lost in her sobs.

"Take me prisoner if you want!" said the father. "But leave my family alone!"

His plea fell on deaf ears. The leader smiled fiercely and maliciously, revealing his dark, crooked teeth. With tremendous tugs he tore off the girl's white skirt.

Again she thought of resisting and fleeing, but the fear that they would shoot her to death right there in front of her parents made her stop. She felt the men's stares lacerating her virgin body like lightning bolts.

The leader came forward and pushed her toward a room which, by chance, was the girl's own room, daintily adorned with pictures of children, dolls and other things that she had collected and kept with her most intimate and beautiful childhood secrets.

The father, meanwhile, was consumed with rage and the mother was crying silently. Neither of them could comprehend how it was possible that such an injustice could be committed against weak and humble people.

"My God, how can this be possible! What have we done to make You abandon us?" thought the mother, torn apart by immense pain as she listened to the man struggling to overcome the resistance and screams of the girl. The mother lost consciousness and collapsed.

The father, face down on the floor, bit his lips until they bled, unable to defend his loved ones. He remembered scenes from his daughter's childhood, when he and his wife played happily with their little girl, never imagining that one horrible day fate would betray them.

The last one came out of the bedroom. They took the father away, leaving behind the disgraced daughter and the mother, still unconscious on the floor.

That had happened yesterday. Today, sitting in the garden, a few steps from the hammock, as he and his companion slipped slowly into a deep sleep, the leader remembered the young, brown body of the schoolgirl. The third man came outside and, noticing that the others were sleeping, went back to watch over the entrance to the house.

2

The old man got out of the hammock and went over to the fountain. He splashed his face with the cool, clear water. Four beings attired in brilliant tunics observed him silently. He stopped before them ceremoniously, and said:

"Balám-Quitzé will descend with the fall of night... His mantle of light will cleanse our race of all its pain..."

The men awakened at the sound of the old man's voice. They listened with great attention from where they sat but were not able to understand what was happening.

"Balám-Acab and Mahucutáh will appear on the horizon. With immense tongues of fire they will purify the earth of all the blood that has been shed, the sacred blood of our sacrificed ancestors..."

The old man's words became spirals of multi-colored crystal which ascended skyward, breaking up with a thunderous noise. The yard was filled with a heavenly light and a delicate rain of tiny butterflies covered the garden.

The men took out their weapons and shot at the old man. The one who was keeping watch at the doorway came running and joined in the attack. They emptied their weapons, and were astonished when they realized that they had not harmed anyone.

"The mountain range will tremble and from within Iqui-Balám will emerge... His hosts will destroy all traces of imperial races... The monuments that have enslaved our species and confused our understanding will perish..."

They reloaded their weapons and attacked the assembly again. The old man was speaking and the personages listened attentively, as if the men and the shooting did not exist.

"The conquest of our empire will be complete and irreversible... It will include domination to the limits of the universe, from the brilliance of the sun to the radiance of the moon... Then will our gods return and ascend to their thrones. Our lineage will again assume

control over the day and the night, over the rain and the winds...
And it will be the beginning of a new age of splendor..."

Holding scepters of light, the four beings moved forward. As they spoke, their proclamations rose skyward, breaking into multicolored rain.

When the assembly concluded, the three men ran to the door and fled terrified into the street.

"The subversives are coming!" they shouted. "Prepare yourselves!"

People walked right by without paying any attention to their frantic screams.

3

The usual calm reigned in the garden. Water flowed from the fountain and fell into the pool which reflected a clear blue sky. The birds had escaped from their cages. The old man's body remained motionless in the hammock. The statue of Gucumatz, imposing and impassive, projected its gaze of millenarian stone over the garden.

That night, when the sun had hidden behind the mountain, a rain of tiny stars illuminated the earth. The wind let loose in gusts whose invisible hands ripped the leaves from the trees and the petals from the flowers. The fragile line of the horizon split into shining points of light which rose to the sky and then, falling to earth, turned into gigantic balls of fire. Volcanoes erupted. Strong earthquakes tore apart the bowels of the planet. Rivers, lakes and seas overflowed. The deluge leveled everything, leaving not a rock upon a rock nor a bone upon a bone.

When the sun rose, its warm rays illuminated the face of the earth, green and rejuvenated. The mountain was covered with tiny white points of light which came to life and descended into the valleys. Then the new man was revealed.

(1986)

*"Who will tell, my child,
what the water holds
with its flowing tail
through its emerald hall?"*

Federico García Lorca

ONCE UPON A RIVER

1

The river nourished the valley with life, love and fantasy. Along its way flowers and trees sprang forth, crops and animals flourished, families and towns expanded...

2

The school bell rang. Micolión and Tomás ran outside, shouted "Recess!" and joined Chepetoño, Tapir and Jacinto.

"Wow, that test was hard."

"If it hadn't been for this, we would've flunked."

Micolión held out a paper folded like an accordion: "The Algebra test. Tapir passed it to me and I passed it to Chepetoño."

Chepetoño: "And I gave it to Jacinto."

Jacinto: "We have the Chemistry one, too. We're going to get an A in every subject."

Tapir: "Cool!"

Tomás: "Aren't you embarrassed? You don't even study because you're off wasting time with Lupe; that woman is getting rich off you guys."

Jacinto: "Lupe is 'rich' with or without us, isn't she, Chepetoño?"

Chepetoño: "Hey, look at him; his mouth is watering."

Micolión: "It's just that Tomás doesn't know a good thing when he sees it."

Chepetoño: "You spend all your time studying, and what for? To get a C? We get A's and enjoy life, isn't that right, Tapir?"

Tapir: "Right!"

Micolión: "Cool!"

Tomás: "One of these days the teacher is going to catch you."

Jacinto challenges him: "So what?"

"Then he'll flunk all of you, and you'll have to repeat the grade, for being so lazy."

Micolión: "No way, Macho Suelto is always drunk or tired from staying up all night."

Chepetoño interrupted: "Tell him about last night, Jacinto, so he can die laughing."

"Do you know who we met in Lupe's house, buttoning up his shirt?"

Tomás: "Who?"

Jacinto: "None other than the Ethics and Civics teacher."

"No, it can't be. That old man isn't strong enough to even carry his books any more."

Micolión: "That's why Lupe said he had fallen asleep on her in bed."

"What a riot!"

Chepetoño: "And that's nothing, when he was leaving he got us mixed up with the sophomores."

Teacher: "I just came to inspect the house, boys. I'm doing a study on urbanism and architecture."

Tapir: "Your fly is open, teacher!"

"And he was so embarrassed he slipped on a mango peel and almost fell; his briefcase crashed to the floor, books and aspirins spilled all over the living room where we were waiting our turn, money in hand, unable to hold back our laughter and Chimbolo, Lupe's husband, had to quiet us down."

"Silence, boys, or the woman can't concentrate."

Tapir: "From the living room we could hear Lupe laughing, and the teacher rushed out without picking up the aspirins, a magazine with pictures of nude women and the semester exams for the sophomores, which we sold to them so they can get A's and we can pay for more visits to Lupe."

Micolión: "What a great night!"

Chepetoño: "Awesome!"

Tomás: "You guys are disgusting; not even the teacher escapes you! What hope is there for our country!"

3

The next day after school Jacinto, Micolión, Chepetoño and Tapir were waiting in the doorway of the school.

"This time we're going, Tomás. Quit acting so stupid."

Tomás: "I have to study for the test tomorrow."

Tapir: "Aren't you a man?"

"I'm more of a man than all of you together. I can handle you, come on, I dare you!"

And the five boys walked down the dusty hill joking like they did every day, travelling the five kilometers of distance that separated the school from the village where they lived.

"Besides, today I have to husk corn and take Chencho a pig that he promised to buy."

Jacinto: "See, now Tomás is a pig vendor."

Micolión: "Since when?"

"Since they killed my dad."

Tapir: "They almost killed my dad, too, but the day of the invasion he was sick and didn't go to the cooperative farm."

Dad: "Look, son, what they call agrarian reform is nothing but lies, because when we *campesinos* arrive to work the land, they shoot us."

Tapir: "That's why now he spends all his time drinking and doesn't want to hear any more about those reforms."

Dad: "Because we *campesinos* always come out losing."

Micolión had climbed a tree and was throwing ripe mangos at them.

"Micolión, you look like a monkey!"

"As if the idiot were a gorilla!"

"Micolión, you pig, leave the mangos alone!"

"Mangos, let Micolión go!"

Suddenly he leapt down from the tree and rushed over to his friends.

"What's wrong, Micolión? Did you see a snake?"

"Tell us, what's the matter?"

"Stop it, be quiet, along the river there, the soldiers are coming, I saw them from the top of the tree, let's run and hide."

Immediately they gathered up their books, jumped over the barbed-wire fence and threw themselves down behind some thick bushes, where they remained motionless, their anxious gazes fixed on the path, whispering. "There comes a truck full of soldiers from the army base."

"The one with the dark glasses is Lieutenant Yuca Santamarta, the rapist."

"He picks on the weak. But one of these days he'll run up against a real man and get what he deserves."

"Be quiet, stupid, or they'll hear us. Look who they've got tied up, Goat Beard, the Spanish teacher."

"Why would they be taking him?"

"Maybe they accused him of being a Communist."

"I wonder if he got a student pregnant. The old man is a skirt-chaser."

When they were sure that the troops were far enough away, they emerged from hiding and went back to the path, stoning birds with their slingshots and cutting fruit with their machetes. They arrived at Valley Crossroad, and again insisted to Tomás:

"Come on, let's go to Lupe's."

Tomás: "I already told you no, you guys go, I have to sell the pig; if I don't there'll be nothing to eat at my house."

"Pig man!"

They shouted and took off running. Tomás picked up some stones and threw them at the jokers.

"One of these days your... is going to rot!"

But why should he shout if they were already so far away? They wouldn't hear him.

4

As soon as he entered the house he noticed the smell of boiled beans and toasted tortillas.

"Hi, Mom."

"Are you hungry?"

"Yes, Mom."

From the other side of the dining room his sister came in.

"How's it going, Chele?"

"Hi, Tomás."

She slipped away toward the bedroom, probably to tell the men who it was that had come in. The steaming plate of rice and beans was waiting on the table next to the stack of tortillas and a chunk of fresh cheese wrapped in green leaves. His mother was sad and in mourning since the death of Virgilio, his father, to which had now been added the worry and fear that the authorities would discover the "boys" who were hiding in the house.

Mother: "They would kill all of us, Tomás; be careful not to say anything to anyone."

Tomás: "Yes, Mom."

The woman went outside to throw some leftover tortillas to the pigs. Chele came out of the bedroom and sat down at the table to eat bits of cheese and scare away the flies. The grief which had remained etched on her face after her father's death had disappeared with the arrival of Cousin Matías, who was gone from the village for a time and then returned leading a group of rebels. Now Chele smiled a lot and talked of strange things, the rights of the people, democracy, liberation, a so-called "popular cause" which Tomás didn't understand, or didn't want to understand, because at the age of sixteen all he wanted was to be a good student.

"To take care of you, Mom, and some day go to the capital and get a good job, study at night at the university and get my degree in agronomy."

He was tired of his sister's same old questions:

"Had he talked to his friends about the men who were hiding in the house?"

"No."

"Had he heard of any strange happenings in the valley?"

"No."

"Had anyone asked him odd questions at school?"

"No, but this afternoon when Micolión, Chepetoño, Jacinto, Tapir and I were coming home from school, we saw Lieutenant Yuca Santamarta and his troops. They had taken Goat Beard, the Spanish teacher, prisoner, and he was all bruised and beaten."

The news surprised Chele, who immediately went into the bedroom to tell the men.

Mother: "Tomasito, eat. Hurry, because you have to take Chencho the fattest pig. That one, look. The one that grunts so much at night, as if he were seeing the devil, and doesn't let us sleep, that very one. Take it to him before it gets too late, son."

Chele emerged, smiling, from the room where the men were hiding, and she sat down at the table.

"What a lot of flies, my God."

Her mother threw her an angry glance which erased her smile. She lowered her head and hid her pretty face behind the thick dark-brown hair which reflected the golden rays of the afternoon sun.

"And you, Tomás, hurry up; don't stuff yourself with so many tortillas. You're starting to look like a pig yourself."

5

They found Lupe's husband in the doorway of the house, eating a ripe mango.

"You're going to enjoy yourselves today, boys; she's fresh, she just took a bath, go on in."

He threw the mango pit into a corner and wiped his mouth on his sleeve.

Micolión: "What do you think, Tomás?"

Tomás: "You bums! You're as degenerate as Lupe and her husband."

"It's hunger, Tomás."

"It's ignorance, Chepetoño."

Tomás: "The man is drunk all day, and the woman working to support his habit and five children, all from different fathers, and you bums taking advantage of others' misfortune."

"What the hell, Pig Man, you talk like that priest they butchered for preaching more than he should have."

"If you keep on with your old man's sermons, we're going to report you to the Patrol."

"You talk bad about Lupe because you haven't tried her. Maybe you don't even like women; you don't even flirt with the girls at school."

Tomás: "There is one, but she's shy."

"Who is it? Micolión's sister?"

"No."

"Chepetoño's cousin?"

"No, that one."

"Which one?"

"That one, with the blue skirt."

"Esperanza?"

"Yes, but don't point."

"Chapupa's sister?"

"Yes, but don't say it so loud."

"The one who lives in La Arada?"

"Yes, man, yes."

"She's pretty."

Tomás: "But she's shy."

"And who wouldn't be? With that face of yours, you scare all the girls!"

"You're out of luck, Tomás, because Lieutenant Yuca Santamarta has his eye on Esperanza; he's really after her."

"And they say that Yuca Santamarta, where he puts his eye, he puts his claws."

"So if you try to get close to her you'll have to deal with the Lieutenant."

"But since we're your friends, we'll help you. She always walks with some girlfriends. We'll walk with them when we get out of school today."

"Jacinto knows one of them: Tila."

Tomás: "Then you guys go on ahead with the friends and I'll stay behind with Esperanza."

"Good plan!"

"We're all agreed then?"

"For sure!"

When the bell rang, they were ready to join the girls.

Tapir: "We'll walk you home; the road is dangerous."

At first they said no, but the boys insisted and the plan worked.

"Well, all right, but no touching or pawing or anything."

Micolión assured them: "We just want to walk with you so nothing bad will happen to you."

Jacinto: "Because the roads are full of criminals who mistreat women."

Marta: "Oh yes, how awful!"

Tila: "Several girls from La Arada have been raped."

Rosenda: "Oh my God, don't say that!"

Panchita: "Dear God!"

Tapir thought: "What crazy girls!"

But, meanwhile, they had managed to walk on ahead and leave Tomás and Esperanza alone, and Chepetoño and Jacinto were congratulating each other, in whispers, for the success of their plan. Talking about any old thing just to distract the girls, they reached Valley Crossroad and took the path which was known in the valley as "Lupe's road."

Marta: "That's the house of that dirty woman."

Tila: "Don't point; a curse could fall on you."

Micolión and his friends laughed and whispered to each other: "If these crazy girls only knew that Lupe is the most delicious thing in the world."

"One of these days we'll get these girls, what do you say?"

"Agreed!"

But they weren't, because even after three weeks of walks, jokes, and compliments, the girls responded with the same old song: "No touching or pawing or anything."

6

Mother: "Chele left yesterday early in the morning with the men and she hasn't come back. I'm not going to have anything to do with her anymore; she can make her own decisions; she's an adult. One of these days she's going to get pregnant or the authorities are going to arrest her, but it doesn't matter to me anymore. You just eat, Tomás, and then go to bed; I'm going to Locha's house, maybe I'll get to talk to Virgilio."

"Don't go, Mom, that old woman is a witch."

"Just listen to what this kid says! Come on, respect people; Locha is a saint!"

"My father died; not even the devil can bring him back."

Tomás insisted on going with her.

"To take care of you, Mom; the road is dangerous."

They found the old woman talking to herself, dressed in black, her hair messy and dirty like a bird's nest, her toothless mouth stinking of garlic, lighting candles to the images of Saint Caralampio and all the other saints who hung on the smoke-stained walls of the small adobe house, framed under broken glass and full of spider webs and dead flies, crickets, and cockroaches which were mixed and jumbled together with scapularies, ribbons, and medals.

"Tomás, don't point at the saints or your finger will fall off!"

Locha was beating her chest and making labyrinthine signs in front of her dark, wrinkled face with her bony hands, talking between long sighs to all the bearded, curly-haired saints, saints of all races, nailed to crosses of different sizes and designs, small female saints, thin ones and fat ones, smiling with golden halos suspended over their heads, holding in their arms plump, naked, blue-eyed children in whose hands rested globes, little houses, and multi-colored crosses. Locha's house was the religious temple of the valley, where in exchange for a few pesos or a chicken you could talk to souls in heaven, purgatory or hell.

Mother: "Wait for me outside, Tomás."

"Okay, Mom."

The woman knelt and crossed herself.

"Leave, because they don't allow minors in here."

"Okay, Mom."

He sat down on a rock just outside the door, and began to draw houses in the dirt with his machete. Just as well, because Locha terrified him; what if she gave him the "test of purity" and left him bewitched or made a snake grow in his stomach that would eat his intestines, heart and liver and turn him into a reptile?

His friends laughed at all that.

Tapir: "Nothing but superstitions!"

Jacinto: "That old woman is a witch."

Chepetoño: "Everyone in the valley is afraid of that old lady."

Tapir: "She's made a pact with the devil."

Micolión: "They should burn her alive."

Tomás: "People come to see her from other towns and even from the capital, because they say she's a saint, she cures people who have cancer and leprosy; she makes drunks hate liquor, and makes men love women to the point of being their slaves. She makes girls get rich, handsome boyfriends, and communicates with the dead even if their souls are suffering in purgatory, she makes the blind see, the deaf speak, and one-handed people's hands grow back!"

Tapir: "Those are nothing but stories told by ignorant people!"

Tomás' mother came out of the house holding a handful of candles and a bottle of "Spirit of Sugarcane" with black water and small red grains that looked like fish eyes.

"To sprinkle on the floor of the bedroom so that the sun and moon may protect Matías and the boys; this candle so Chele won't get pregnant, this one so the authorities won't find the house in case they do suspect something, this one so the pigs will get fat..."

"And how much did you pay for all that, Mom?"

"Five pesos, but I didn't get to talk to your dad because Locha couldn't find him anywhere in the universe even though she looked for him in heaven, in hell, and in purgatory; there was no sign of him anywhere. But she told me to come back the third night of the full moon and bring a fat toad."

All of that made Tomás feel afraid and sick to his stomach.

"Hurry up, son, don't fall behind or it will get dark and we'll see the Headless Horseman who scared Chele one Good Friday when she took a bath and ate pork. Just for being foolish, as if she didn't know that is a mortal sin. I warned her. Look, daughter, that is a sin. But these young people are stubborn, my God! When are they going to learn? They think they know everything. And you, Tomás, hurry up; it's already getting dark and I'm starting to hear strange noises, as if Lucifer were scraping the tree trunks with his long fingernails."

7

The news spread throughout the valley that an army truck with twenty dead soldiers had been found.

Jacinto: "They say the guerrillas ambushed them."

Tapir: "Now for sure all hell's going to break loose in the villages."

Micolión: "They're going to sweep through the whole valley."

Tomás thought about his sister, the bedroom at their house, his mother, the pigs.

"All for the popular cause."

"And what's the popular cause?"

"Explain it to us, Tomás, since you read so much."

He didn't know, but he would ask his sister.

"And why your sister?"

"What does she know about these things?"

"Because..."

But he contained himself, and thought: "I almost put my foot in it..."

Then he took a deep breath.

"Well, because she reads more than I do, and don't ask me such stupid questions!"

"Okay, Tomás, don't get mad, we're friends, remember?"

"If you get mad we won't go with you today so you can flirt with Esperanza."

"It doesn't matter; she's too shy. After so many walks and stories she won't even let me hold her hand."

"Don't give up; she's just playing hard to get."

Esperanza: "Inside I'm dying for him, Panchita."

Rosenda: "Ask him to write a poem for you; they say he's something of a poet."

Tila: "Maybe he'll give you a present."

Esperanza: "A present? I'm not expecting gifts from anyone; I'm not selfish."

Jacinto: "Little by little, take it slow, Tomás."

Tapir: "Don't lose heart, friend."

Jacinto: "Hang in there; when school's out today we'll follow them again and go back on the attack."

And after some time not only Esperanza and Tomás withdrew from the others, but also Marta and Chepetoño, Panchita and Micolión, Rosenda and Tapir; even Tila and Jacinto resolved their differences and walked in front of the others.

Once when they were approaching Valley Crossroad there was a cloudburst, and they ran to take shelter under the trees and bushes. The couples separated from each other, and when the rain finally stopped, no one was in a hurry to return to the path.

An hour later they left their hiding places, all very content, and laughing.

Tapir: "Let's promise that we'll keep this a secret."

Tomás: "And that none of the ten of us will ever forget the blessed rainstorm which brought us such happiness."

Esperanza: "Yes, Tomás, that blessed afternoon when we loved each other for the first time."

Micolión: "See? She finally gave in."

Tila: "Like Panchita was telling you, Esperanza: just be patient; God knows what He is doing."

Rosenda and Tila: "Amen!"

8

"The third night of the full moon when I took Locha the fat toad in a bag, she still couldn't find Virgilio."

Locha: "It must be that when they killed him they threw his body in the river and it was eaten by fish and snakes and his soul was left stuck in the rocks at the bottom."

"That's nothing but nonsense, Mom. Please don't waste money paying Locha anymore; my dad died and that's it. It would be better for the priest here in the valley to dedicate a mass so Dad's soul can rest in peace."

"But, Tomás, didn't you know that the church is closed because the priest left to join the guerrillas?"

"No, Mom, the priest was killed."

"I don't really know what happened, but Chele is with them, too. They say that she was promoted to commander and that she's been seen training peasants to assault troops and burn ranches. That's all we needed, for your sister to go off to the mountains to fight."

"That's her choice, Mom. She's an adult now."

"And the only reason she hasn't gotten pregnant is because I lit one of the candles that Locha prescribed. I'm sure that if your father were alive, she wouldn't be involved in all that. Is that all she went to school for, to learn bad habits and strange things?"

"School is very important, Mom. They teach you to read and write; just learning that opens up a whole new world."

"Just eat and don't be talking about those things, Tomás; and don't you get involved in that mess."

But lately he was only thinking about Esperanza. The memory of her rosy, warm breasts gave him chills.

"Finish eating, Tomás, don't sit there staring at the ceiling like you're hypnotized; what, are you sick?"

"No, Mom."

"Do you have a fever?"

"No, Mom."

"Hm. Maybe you have worms in your stomach."

"No, Mom; nothing's wrong with me," and he thought: "What I do have right now is an irresistible urge to be with you, Esperanza; you've got a spell over me."

"Maybe you have a tapeworm in your stomach that's eating you from the inside."

And he thought: "If you knew, Mom, that what has me feeling this way are Esperanza's plump, soft legs, her big brown eyes, her chestnut hair, her red lips, her pink cheeks, her kisses of honey."

"When I take Locha an armadillo later, I'll ask her for one of her miraculous ointments to rub on your back, and it'll get rid of whatever is bothering you, because you're very pale and you don't want to study or even eat anymore."

"I'm fine, Mom. Don't worry."

Tapir: "You look just like you did the first time we took you to Lupe's, remember, guys?"

Micolión: "Remember, Chepetoño, how Tomás was screaming 'I feel like I'm going to die!'"

"And Lupe was laughing."

"And Chimbolo, with the bottle of booze in his hand: 'You're dying but from pleasure!'"

"Tomás came stumbling out, with his hair standing up, looking so pale."

"And after that he kept begging us to lend him money and asking us to go, because then he had more energy than Micolión."

"His mom was so worried that Locha prescribed some strange liquid for him."

Mother: "For you to gargle with, Tomasito, every three hours, because you're so thin you look like a skeleton."

Chepetoño: "But by then it wasn't Lupe anymore; it was Esperanza."

And he thought: "It's the best thing in the world, Mom."

9

They were joking and pushing each other around in the schoolyard when suddenly a man on horseback appeared in front of them.

"Who is the imbecile who's after my daughter? Who is this Micolión? Be a man and tell me who you are because I'm going to give you what you deserve!"

The furious man made his machete whistle in the air as he spurred his enormous, spirited, neighing black horse. The man's foaming lips trembled in anger.

"Which of you is Micolión?"

The boys looked at each other, pretending they didn't understand, and asked each other indifferently:

"Do you know who Micolión is?"

"No."

"And you?"

"No."

"And you?"

"No."

"No."

"No."

Tapir pointed to Chepetoño, who appeared older than the others.

"Ask Professor Pérez."

The horseman, unable to control his fury, hurled the question.

"Professor, do you know?"

Chepetoño frowned and imitated Goat Beard, the Spanish teacher.

"Pardon me, do I know what?"

"Who is Micolión?"

"What's that?"

"The son of a bitch, forgive me, Professor, who is after my daughter!"

"And who is your daughter?"

"Panchita Linares."

"Hm, well no, I don't know who she is."

"And Micolión?"

"No, sir. I don't know who Micolión is either. There are no students with names of animals here, only people with Christian names like you and me."

"Well, you all tell that Micolión, or whatever the hell his name is, that he'd better watch himself, because if I catch him bothering my daughter I'll cut him up and drink his blood!"

He dug the spurs into his huge horse, making it rear and snort, and took off out of the schoolyard as if possessed by the devil.

Micolión: "Who is Micolión?"

And they all started laughing and Panchita winked at him from the corridor where she had hidden behind a post. The other girls went over to her and they began to whisper and laugh about the infuriated horseman.

"Now you're screwed, Micolión; now you can't go with Panchita anymore because the old man will kill you."

"It's because he wants to marry her off to a rich man, not to an ugly, broke guy like you."

"You'd better look for a different girlfriend."

Micolión: "If her father is against it, I'll just steal her."

"But Panchita won't run away with you; she's not stupid."

Micolión: "She sure will. We've sworn to love each other forever; we're getting married."

"This sounds serious."

"I'd never be stupid enough to get married at 17."

"Without any money."

"Without an education."

"Without a job."

"I wouldn't do it either."

"Girls are just for having a good time."

"I'll get married after I've graduated as an agronomist."

"I will when my dad dies and I inherit his property."

Micolión: "But I'm in love with Panchita."

"Love is one thing; real problems are another. It's best if you just forget about her."

"No, she and I love each other, and if her father objects, we'll flee to the other side of the river, where my aunt lives."

"But then it would be worse because the old man will look for you and if he finds you he'll kill both of you."

"They say he's really mean, and that once he defeated five National Guardsmen, all by himself."

"Remember, Micolión, that Panchita also has three brothers who are just as mean as their father."

"Their nickname is The Tailors, because if they don't like you they'll do their famous 'Vest Cut' on you."

"What that means, Micolión, is that they cut off your head and arms."

But in spite of all the advice from his friends, Micolión didn't come to school the next day, nor did Panchita, and throughout the valley the news circulated that they had run away together.

Tapir: "What a stupid thing for Micolión to do; he didn't even say goodbye to his friends."

Chepetoño: "As if our friendship weren't a sacred thing."

Tomás: "But love is blind, and I would do the same with you, Esperanza, if we were ever forced to separate."

Esperanza: "So would I, because my love for you grows stronger each day, and sometimes I feel like I'm going crazy because you're always on my mind. I never stop dreaming that I'm holding you against my chest, lying in this hiding place in the shade of this huge fig tree. I dream that we're always happy like at this moment."

The other couples were waiting on the path, whistling like birds.

"Let's go! It's getting late!"

Esperanza and Tomás emerged from their hiding place, brushing off each other's clothes, holding hands, while the afternoon sun covered them with a delicately warm orange veil.

On the other side of the river, Panchita and Micolión were happy, too, just as their dear friends were every afternoon near Valley Crossroad, on the way home from school.

10

The violence of the civil war gripped towns and villages. Soldiers and guardsmen appeared dead on the roads and floating in the river. Peasants died at co-op farms as they cultivated the land. In the schoolyard, the tortured body of Professor Goat Beard was found.

One afternoon when the boys and their girlfriends were on the way home from school, near Valley Crossroad, they met a group of soldiers led by Lieutenant Yuca Santamarta, who jumped down from the truck and blocked their way, furious, spitting dust. The soldiers aimed their long rifles at the couples, their fingers on the trigger awaiting the order to fire. Yuca Santamarta approached Tomás and looked at him scornfully.

"How about that? We're both after the same woman! Don't you know, you snot-nosed brat, that what's mine is mine and I'll decide what's yours?"

He grabbed Esperanza roughly and pulled her over next to him. She threw the lieutenant a hateful look.

"I don't know who you are. And I'm not yours, either."

She returned to Tomás' side and put her arms around him.

Tapir thought: "You just feel brave because you have all those troops at your command."

"I'll love Tomás until the day I die."

Yuca Santamarta's face clouded momentarily and then revealed a cruel vengeful smile.

"Well then, let the sweethearts die!"

The other girls implored:

"No, for God's sake, no!"

"They haven't hurt anyone!"

Yuca Santamarta: "Loving what is mine is a crime!"

Their protests just increased the lieutenant's rage.

"So, you are rebels, too? Then you will die for being disrespectful to the authorities!"

He raised his arm and shouted: "Fire!" And at that moment, the trees, bushes and rocks of Valley Crossroad vomited smoke and long, hard bursts of gunfire. Yuca Santamarta was the first one to fall, headfirst into the dust, followed by his soldiers, while the friends took off running, thanking Saint Valentine for protecting them and saving them from the jaws of the ferocious Yuca Santamarta.

11

Tila began to miss school, had a lot of pain in her back, became very thin, lost her appetite, and was vomiting blood.

Jacinto: I don't know what's wrong with her; she can't even walk.

"Maybe you got her pregnant, Jacinto."

"Her mother went to consult Locha, and the old witch gave her ointments and strange-colored drinks, Tomás. I want to see her but her mother gives all kinds of excuses."

Mother: "Tila doesn't want anyone to see her in the condition that she's in, especially you, Jacinto, because she loves you so much. She's embarrassed for you to see her sick."

"I already talked to her dad and asked for her hand, formally."

Father: "Of course, Jacinto, when Tila gets better the two of you will be married and will be very happy together."

"I hope everything will turn out all right; what do you guys think?"

Tapir: "Everything will turn out just great, isn't that right, guys?"

Chepetoño: "That's right."

Tomás: "Of course."

Tapir: "Yeah!"

But the young man still cried over not being able to see his girlfriend.

Jacinto: "To tell her how much I love her, and to get better, and that we should get married. To have a lot of children. For me to work like a horse from dawn to dusk on the farm although they'll pay me a miserable salary like they do everyone else. To build a little house and live happily ever after."

His friends consoled him on the river bank where they got together to drink moonshine. Jacinto drank like a bottomless pit and cried profusely.

Jacinto: "Where are you, my dear Tila, my corn field in flower?"

"Don't cry, man."

"Crying won't fix anything."

"I bet tomorrow she'll come to school smiling and full of energy and charm."

But Tila didn't come back to school. Nor did Jacinto go to school anymore. His friends would find him drunk on the bank of the river. The days passed, and Tila's family gave the same excuses.

Mother: "Tomorrow, Jacinto."

Father: "Yes, tomorrow for sure, she'll be better."

Tomorrow came.

Mother: "Tomorrow for sure, she's getting better already."

Father: "Tila will be ready tomorrow."

Mother: "Yes, tomorrow you two will be able to talk about wedding plans, about children, about a home."

But the anxiously awaited tomorrow never came, because the boiled remedies, the dark liquids, candles and ointments of old Locha didn't have any effect. Tila grew more fearful and strange every day. Her body became deformed.

Tomás: "Tila's younger sister told me that Tila doesn't want to see or talk to anyone. That she stays locked up in her room day and night without eating. She hates noise and light. She only lets Locha enter her room."

Chepetoño: "Her other sister says that Locha takes her toads and frogs, pig and cat ears, chicken feet, snakeskin, yellow cherry juice, powder of eye of newt, leaves and mushrooms, and that Tila swallows all that and at the same time eats spiders, cockroaches and crickets, since nothing else seems to satisfy her strange appetite."

Tapir: "They say that when Locha goes into her room they hear screams of horror, curses and the noise of plates and pots crashing against the wall, and that the old woman comes out all scratched and bleeding as if she had escaped death by no less than a miracle. But she's stubborn."

Locha: "Tomorrow I'm going to cure Tila, you'll see. Because I'm going to bring her the medicine of all medicines."

And the next day the whole family waited with great longing.

Tomás: "They saw her go into the room with a black gourd bowl. She entered and the noise, the crashing and screaming, began again."

Chepetoño: "You could hear howling and hellish screams throughout the whole village."

Tapir: "Finally the noise stopped and calm returned to Tila's house. And as the family and neighbors waited anxiously, Locha still did not come out of Tila's room."

Mother: "I entered the room to see what was happening."

Father: "And she immediately came running out, screaming and crying, horrified."

Mother: "I didn't find Locha. And what was there in the room wasn't my daughter but a hairy monster, with claws, talons and long teeth. When it saw me, it jumped on me."

Tomás: "She wanted to eat her own mother."

Chepetoño: "And poor Jacinto, crushed, has never recovered from the great disappointment."

Tapir: "Not even the long drinking binges console him."

Jacinto: "What happened to my Tila, my God? Maybe someone who was jealous of our love put a curse on her."

Tomás: "Please don't cry anymore, Jacinto. You'll see your Tila tomorrow."

Mother: "Yes, tomorrow, for sure."

12

The three friends accompanied their girlfriends to La Arada, and on the way home, a huge cloud of dust suddenly appeared before them.

Tomás: "What's that?"

The boys took out their machetes, ready to defend themselves.

Tapir: "Let's get out of here, Tomás; it might be the devil."

From among the clouds of dust there came macabre laughter that echoed through the whole valley. Suddenly, the dust cloud disappeared.

Chepetoño: "Look, it's Yuca Santamarta!"

Yuca Santamarta: "You're going to hell with me now, Tomás. For stealing Esperanza from me."

The lieutenant's eyes gave off fire. He advanced toward Tomás, who was petrified, open-mouthed, unable to speak.

"Make the sign of the cross at him!"

"Don't just stand there; he's going to take you away!"

"Don't let him take you!"

Chepetoño and Tapir were attacking Yuca Santamarta with their machetes, but the weapons went right through him without causing him any harm.

Chepetoño: "You'll never have your way!"

Tapir: "You aren't going to take Tomás!"

But they were unable to stop him. Chepetoño took one of his friend's hands, making the sign of the cross with his fingers and showing it to Yuca Santamarta, who was about to take him away, but when he saw the cross he fell back screaming in pain, and moved away in a cloud of dust.

Yuca Santamarta: "I'll be back for you because my soul will never rest until I take you with me to hell!"

He disappeared laughing raucously; the noise made Tomás open his eyes, and he woke up crying. His mother was holding his hand and had made a cross with his fingers.

"You fell asleep with your hand over your heart, Tomasito. You were having a nightmare. Drink this lemonade. Pray three Hail Marys and lie face down, then you'll sleep well. I'm going to light this candle to Saint Caralampio so the bad spirits will go away."

Chepetoño: "I dreamed exactly the same thing last night!"

Tapir: "I did too. What a strange coincidence that the three of us had the same nightmare."

Tomás: "Maybe Yuca Santamarta didn't die in the shooting."

"Or maybe he died but his soul is wandering as punishment for all the evil things he did in his life."

"From now on we'd better stick together on the road."

"Let's all walk together and be ready to take out our machetes and make the sign of the cross."

"Let's wear a scapulary. That way Yuca Santamarta won't catch us unprepared and take us with him to hell."

13

They went down to the river to meet Jacinto, whom they usually found there drinking moonshine.

"No sign of Jacinto."

"Where do you think he could be?"

"Maybe he went to see Tila."

"Maybe she got better."

Chepetoño waded into the river and pulled out a big bag tied to a rock with a rope. He unwrapped a drinking gourd full of moonshine and they went to sit down and drink in the shade of an enormous fig tree.

"Tomás, Tapir, look at that!"

"What is it?"

"It looks like an animal!"

"It's big and hairy!"

"Move it with a stick."

"No, it might bite me! You move it."

"Don't be afraid Chepetoño; that's what you have your machete for."

"It might be a gorilla."

"Don't be a fool, Tapir; there are no gorillas in El Salvador."

They approached the thing, machetes in hand, and Tomás poked it with a stick.

"Look how big it is!"

"What kind of beast is this?"

"It's hairy and has long fangs."

"Let's just get out of here; it might be the devil."

"Don't be afraid; it doesn't even move. It looks like it's dead."

"It looks like a big monkey."

"Don't poke it anymore, Tomás."

"It really stinks!"

"It's rotten."

"Leave it alone, Tomás, it might wake up and eat us alive."

"Wait, don't be such chickens. Grab some sticks and help me turn it over."

"Just a minute, I'm going to get a stick."

"Okay, let's all push at the same time. One, two, three, now!"

"Look, it was on top of Jacinto!"

They were shocked to see their friend Jacinto lying on the ground, face up, with a big smile on his face as if he were sleeping happily and dreaming of being in heaven.

"Wake up, Jacinto!"

They pushed at his body with their sticks.

"Oh no, he's dead!"

They took off running, to tell Jacinto's parents and the other residents of the village who, hearing the news, armed themselves with machetes, sticks, stones and knives, and followed Tomás, Chepetoño and Tapir who ran ahead. They reached the tree near the river bank but they found neither the animal nor Jacinto's body. The boys swore that they had seen them with their own eyes, but no one believed their words, and all the people returned to their homes, some of them disappointed at not seeing the monster and others angry at the supposed deceit. That was the last time the three boys saw their friend Jacinto. And since then Tila's family had no news of her, either. In the valley the rumors were that Jacinto had kidnapped Tila to take her away to strange lands, on the other side of the river.

Tomás: "Now there are only three of us left."

Chepetoño: "Three friends and our three girlfriends."

Tapir: "That's right."

14

When Tomás arrived home after another day at school, he
found his house abandoned. His mother, who usually was waiting
for him with supper on the table at that time of day, was not there
either. Suddenly he noticed that the rooms had been ransacked
and that everything was in a mess, and he immediately thought
the worst.

"They discovered Chele and the men!"

He looked for his mother outside in the yard. His desperation
turned into screams.

"Mom! Chele! Where are you!"

He heard gunshots in the distance. Someone went running
by. He heard loud noises and ran out to the main road. He could
not believe what he saw: The inhabitants of the village were running away desperately, as if fleeing from something terrifying in
the midst of screams, sobs and curses.

"Run to the river!"

Women and men were carrying their children. Children were
crying, women moaning. Elderly people were falling and dragging
themselves along the ground. Suddenly he heard a familiar voice.

Esperanza: "Tomás, run or they'll kill you!"

He ran to his girlfriend, who was waiting for him, terrorized,
on the road.

"What's going on? What is all this about?"

"They've invaded the village! They're killing anyone they
find!"

A woman who was carrying three children tripped and fell in
the dust. The little ones rolled on the ground and cried. Tomás left
Esperanza and helped the woman up. The shots sounded closer.
The people were running in a desperate stampede, pushing each
other.

"We're close to the river!"

"The river will save us!"

Helicopters flew over the trees, vomiting bombs and bullets. Homes were devoured by flames. The stampede finally reached the banks and the people threw themselves into the water. But the bullets were accurate. The river was incapable of protecting them. Tomás and Esperanza were left locked in an embrace, near a large rock, sprayed with bullets. Chepetoño and Rosenda met the same fate, as did Tapir and Panchita. Hundreds of inhabitants perished. Some of them survived to tell the story.

15

Mercedes: "I was in the river for a long time, next to some children. A five-year-old boy kept begging me to take him out of the water, but I knew that if he got out they would kill him. Upriver, there were a lot of dead people. Almost all my family were shot... They were killing women and children.

"We began to run when we saw that they were surrounding us. The ones they caught, even the children, they tied up. They tied up my husband. They did the same with my daughters, a 14-year-old and a 10-year-old. Of those I was carrying when I fled I was able to save only my two-year old. They killed the others when we were fleeing.

"When I got to the river, they shot me, in the hand and the leg, and I fell, wounded, with my child. I stayed still, between two rocks. The river was full of dead bodies. When the men came up to me, I played dead, praying to God that my child wouldn't cry, because they would kill us. But they kept going.

"Later another group of men passed by with about 50 prisoners, and they killed them all: men, women and children.

"They killed three of my children, my son who was 12, my daughter who was 14, and my five-year-old son. As we were fleeing, my son kept telling me that we should help the dead people, the children whose heads they had cut off.

"That river, believe me, was white with dead bodies."

16

Eduardo: "A group of us were running. And those who got desperate threw themselves into the river, trying to get to the other side. Some did get out on the other side, but others didn't, because the bullets reached them. I was with five of my children, running along the river bank. My wife was behind us with another child, but I don't know exactly on which side or how far behind she was.

"Finally I jumped in to cross the river and I took three of the children to the other side, and then I returned for the other two. The men were getting closer. And it was then that my three-year-old daughter became desperate, seeing that I was swimming away from her, and she threw herself into the water. I couldn't stand to see that the children I had already taken across were coming back and the men were going to kill us. And I didn't know what to do in the middle of the river, because I didn't want to let my daughter drown, but I also needed to get to the others who were waiting for me to help them cross.

"Luckily my other children stopped my daughter and I was able to save the other two who had already jumped in because the men were really close to them already.

"But my wife was still back on the other side, with one of our daughters. I didn't have time to get them across... because the hail of bullets didn't let me...

"I went on with the five children to a village where we would have been ambushed were it not for a boy who warned us. Then it occurred to me to hide the children in the bushes. We slept there that night and I had nothing with which to cover the children. I took off my shirt to protect my daughter from the swarms of mosquitoes. The insects ate me and the other four children all night long. But I had to cover the youngest girl so that she wouldn't cry, because then they would have discovered us.

"It wasn't until the afternoon of the next day that we managed to reach the home of some peasants who gave us food and clothing for the children."

17

Ricardo: "The group of people with whom I was running toward the river began to flee from the village early in the morning. But we didn't jump into the river right away. We ran a long way along the river bank under intense gunfire which killed several in our group. Finally we managed to cross to the other side and we were saved.

"When the massacre finally ended that afternoon, the men left, and the huge number of dead remained there. I saw that they drowned the children they didn't shoot. Others they threw into the air and shot them as they fell. Many adults who didn't know how to swim drowned because the river was deep that day."

18

Tiburcio: "I and some others were saved only because God is great. Because most of the inhabitants of the village are dead. There are the bones of the dead. There are so many of them that they don't fit in my mind.

"That day we all felt pity. The strongest among us cried. Because there were tombs of dead children all along the river."

19

María: "As soon as they got to the village they started killing. They were shooting low with two helicopters. They had arrived early in the morning with trucks. They were chasing the people so that they would flee toward the river. They were taking money from the dead bodies. They killed my brother Juan, who was 27, right there. He left four children.

"I don't know how I was saved. When they overtook me I was lying in the river, wounded, among cadavers, protecting my little son. My five-year-old son was already dead upriver.

"I was all bloody. Some men went by and one of them said: These are dead already. And they kept on going, chasing another group. I stayed there, absolutely still, until the next day. Some peasants who were inspecting the river found me half dead. They took me and my little son out of the river.

"There were so many, many, dead. I remember that they killed don Angel in the village. He was an old man. They assassinated don Chepe and five others who were at his house at that moment; they didn't leave anyone alive. The same thing with don Martín and four others at his house. Don Payén and his 18-year-old daughter. Celestino and Paco. They killed Ernestina along with her three children. One of them, Rubencito, they shot to death; they shot him twice and then cut off his testicles.

"There was a disgusting number of dead people that day. The river was full of cadavers which the current then began to carry downstream. We counted twenty-eight in one place and downstream it was even fuller. There were places where you couldn't see the bodies because the grass was high.

"After the massacre they burned the houses. They were going around as if they were possessed by the devil, setting the houses on fire. Luckily, mine didn't burn. The massacre was horrible. The people fled with nothing. There were parents who had a lot of children, but at the moment they fled they could only carry the little ones. The older ones didn't escape.

"They killed many children. I saw with my own eyes when they killed three of them on the bank of the river. They split another one's head open. He must have been 14 or 15 years old. The next day I found two who died right together, their arms around each other."

20

Many years later, a horseman became lost in the valley and after three days of wandering, overwhelmed by exhaustion, hunger and thirst, he finally found the river.

Voices emanated from the water, singing the tragedy of hundreds of unfortunate souls who once inhabited that region, and one ill-fated day, fleeing from persecution, threw themselves into the river where they died riddled with bullets.

Hearing the sad story, horse and rider refused to drink the water and chose instead to die of thirst.

21

The same waters that once were filled with blood and death became messengers of life and continued nourishing the valley with love and fantasy. Along its way flowers and trees again sprang forth, crops and animals flourished, families and towns expanded.

(1980 - 1996)

**Historical facts which served as
the basis for "Once Upon a River":**

Sumpul River Massacre, May 14, 1980: Minimum of 350 victims. Las Aradas, Chalatenango.

El Mozote Massacre, December 11, 1981: Minimum of 200 victims. Morazán.

El Calabozo Massacre, August 22, 1982: Minimum of 200 victims. Amatitán River, San Vicente.

Documentation of the facts:

"Sumpul," testimonies of survivors gathered by reporters Manuel Torres Calderón, Ursula Ferdinand and Gabriel Sanhueza. Brochure of the Central American University Confederation. CSUCA. July, 1980.

"De la locura a la esperanza - La guerra de 12 años en El Salvador" ("From Insanity to Hope - The 12-year war in El Salvador"). Report of the Truth Commission for El Salvador. United Nations. San Salvador - New York. 1992-1993.

EPILOGUE

Human misery poses a challenge for the writer: to seek a way to reflect reality, however harsh it may be, and, at the same time, create a work of art capable of captivating the reader.

One way to confront the challenge is, perhaps, to add a certain fantasy to reality, so that the work succeeds in seducing the reader, thereby communicating the message to him or her. Literature is also a study of humanity's problems. It attempts to rescue sacred human values, to keep them alive at all costs, with the hope that humanism may finally save the species from succumbing into total chaos. Art, nevertheless, can aspire only to reflect social problems, because resolving them is a political task, not an artistic one.

These stories were written between the years 1979 and 1994. Like the novel *A Shot in the Cathedral*, they were born of a social conflict, the civil war, which took over my work and became not necessarily a social commitment but a natural element, a reflection of that historical reality.

The aesthetic aspect, undoubtedly, represents one of the most difficult dilemmas facing the writer. That is to say, to conceive a work which establishes a balance between social ethics and literary aesthetics, in which the social aspect does not convert it into propaganda and the artistic aspect does not render it a decorative object insensitive to the human drama. For example, the process of documentation of *A Shot in the Cathedral* produced a vast accumulation of data which was impossible to include and which, had it been included, would have made the work a mere imitation of history. And literature is not precisely that, because documenting the exact facts is a function of history. Literature takes certain historical passages and applies an artistic treatment to them, not simply to relate the facts but to shed a certain light upon them and make the human values stand out, to rescue them from oblivion, to revive them so that they do not end up filed away as cold statistics but rather serve as points of reflection; in order that we not forget the atrocities of the past and to keep alive the memory of our heroes. Nor does literature propose to return to the past and stagnate in it, nor to open old wounds, but rather to assure that those wounds scar adequately through study, meditation and understanding of the facts and their consequences, so that we may then come to the firm determination that history must not be repeated because the human cost is too great. In the case of El Salvador, 12 years of civil war, violence, destruction, and more than 75,000 dead.

Several of the literary experiments in this collection, influenced by Mayan mythology and the Popul Vuh, show certain apocalyptic aspects through the example of nature itself which, at times in a drastic manner, renews its elements when they radicalize and threaten to subvert the order and balance of nature. "The Garden of Gucumatz" and "The Insatiable Ones" contain these concepts.

Others were conceived with the deliberate purpose of generating happiness out of tragedy: Life as the product of death. "The Tree of Life," "The Report" and, strangely, "The River Goddess," fit into this category.

The confusion and psychosis which the desolate atmosphere of an armed conflict produces in the inhabitants are themes of "The Deaths of Fortín Coronado" and "Laura's Affliction."

"Photographer of Death" and "The Spirit of Things" are dedicated to the victims of human rights abuses, to the defenders of the universal rights of humankind, and to those who became victims of the very violations they denounced, as did the persons whose names appear at the end of "Photographer of Death," all of them directors of human rights organizations. Quite graphic, sad, and heart-rending, this story is a latent testimony to the violence which shook El Salvador during the civil war.

"The Spirit of Things" attempts to reflect the spiritual power which the word and the personality of Monsignor Romero exercised, even upon those who could not physically see him or were far from him. His abominable assassination was incited by the darkest of motives: the destruction of the spiritual leader and conscience of a people, which represents one of the greatest crimes against humanity. But contrary to the purposes of the assassins, his spirit and his word remain alive, and his light continues to radiate a profound message of peace and hope. Such is the spirit of things. History reminds us that Monsignor Romero was the first Archbishop to be assassinated at the altar in 810 years, since Thomas Becket was stabbed in Canterbury Cathedral by fanatics of Henry II of England on December 29, 1170. Thomas Becket was declared a Holy Martyr two years later. Monsignor Romero was killed on March 24, 1980, and there still is no news of his canonization.

The theme underlying "Clown's Story" is the moral, social and political collapse of a people, seen through the life of a clown and his circus. It plays back and forth between comedy, tragedy, fiction and reality. In a way it is a comical portrait of the artist, because he constantly seeks a way to entertain the world, but the worries of the world are too great and the world does not always have time to listen to his fantasies. One passage from "Clown's Story" reveals the influence of a work by Franz Kafka, which certainly will be discovered by the careful reader.

"Once Upon a River" is new to the second edition, and although its characteristics are really those of a short novel, its concept and theme tie it to the rest of the pieces. The central idea of this work is based on three abominable events of the armed conflict, three occurrences with one common denominator: the massive destruction of human beings, most of them children, elderly people and women. The revelations of some survivors have been incorporated into the text of the story. "Once Upon a River, "like many of the narrations in this collection, combines fiction, historical reality, superstition and testimony. The specific details of the facts are documented in "From Insanity to Hope, "that encyclopedia of the horrors of the Salvadoran civil war. The verses of Federico García Lorca, from the play Blood Wedding, at the beginning of the work inspired certain portions of the story: "Who will tell my child, what the water holds?In this case the waters are those of the Sumpul River in which one of the diabolical events occurred. It is interesting to note that the Spanish poet and playwright was also a victim of the civil war that shook his country during the 1930's and was shot for his ideas on August 19, 1936.

"The Faces of Xipotec" is first introduced in this edition. It is dedicated to the victims of torture, whose physical and emotional suffering in many cases oppresses them throughout their lives. It is also the study of the conflicts which lead the artist to create his works. One paragraph of the last part of the story summarizes this concept: "I never thought that in order to paint that way the artist would have to suffer so much."

"The Insatiable Ones" and "The Garden of Gucumatz" are perhaps the most ambitious experiments herein. They attempt to create a literary work through the unification of two completely opposing situations: a cruel reality and an almost hallucinatory fantasy. I still doubt whether these stories succeeded in crystallizing my aspirations.

"Stories of Civil War" possibly would have been a sufficient title for this collection. Nevertheless, I preferred to include "The Tree of Life" in the title because that composition contains the central ideal of these stories: the end of violence and the resurrection of peace.

About the Author

Mario Bencastro, author and playwright, was born in Ahuachapán, El Salvador, in 1949.

The author's first novel, *A Shot in the Cathedral*, was chosen from among 204 works as a finalist in the "Novedades y Diana International Literary Prize 1989" in Mexico, and was published by Editorial Diana in January, 1990.

In 1994, Mario Bencastro's short novel *The Flight of the Lark* was chosen as a finalist in the "Felipe Trigo Literary Prize," Badajoz, Spain.

In 1988 he wrote and directed *Crossroad*, performed by the Hispanic Cultural Society Theater Group at Thomas Jefferson Theater in Arlington, Virginia, in October of that year. This play was chosen for the "Bicentennial Festival for the Performing Arts" of Georgetown University in April of 1989.

Between 1979 and 1990, Mario Bencastro wrote the collection of short stories *The Tree of Life: Stories of Civil War*, which was published in El Salvador in 1993 by Clásicos Roxsil. Two of these stories, "Photographer of Death" and "Clown's Story," have been adapted for the stage. In addition, the latter was translated into English and included in the international anthologies *Where Angels Glide at Dawn* (HarperCollins, New York, 1990) and *Turning Points* (Nelson Canada, Ontario, 1993). The former is included in *Texto y vida: historia de la literatura hispanoamericana* (Harcourt, Brace, Jovanovich, Texas, 1991) and *Vistas: voces del mundo hispánico* (Prentice Hall, New Jersey, 1995). "The River Goddess" was included in *3 x 5 Worlds Anthology: Salvadoran Short Stories 1962-1992* (UCA Editores, San Salvador, 1994). "The Garden of Gucumatz" was first published by *Hispanic Cultural Review* (George Mason University, Virginia, 1994).

About the Translator

Susan Giersbach Rascón is an attorney who from 1983 to 1989 worked representing Central American refugees, most of them Salvadoran, in their attempts to gain political asylum in the United States. Since 1990 she has taught Spanish at Lawrence University in Appleton, Wisconsin, where she created and taught a course entitled "Art and Social Responsibility: The Work of Mario Bencastro." She has also translated Mr. Bencastro's novel *A Shot in the Cathedral.*